DOCTOR WHO
AND THE
ICE WARRIORS

THE CHANGING FACE OF DOCTOR WHO
The cover illustration portrays the second DOCTOR
WHO whose physical appearance was later altered
by the Time Lords.

DOCTOR WHO
AND THE
ICE WARRIORS

Based on the BBC television serial *The Ice Warriors* by Brian Hayles by arrangement with the BBC

BRIAN HAYLES

Introduction by
MARK GATISS

BOOKS

1 3 5 7 9 10 8 6 4 2

Published in 2012 by BBC Books, an imprint of Ebury Publishing
A Random House Group Company
First published in 1976 by Tandem Publishing Ltd. & Allan Wingate (Publishers) Ltd.

Novelisation copyright © Brian Hayles 1976
Original script © Brian Hayles 1967
Introduction © Mark Gatiss 2012
The Changing Face of Doctor Who and About the Author © Justin Richards 2012
Between the Lines © Steve Tribe 2012

The Random House Group Limited Reg. No. 954009

Addresses for companies within the Random House Group can be found at
www.randomhouse.co.uk

A CIP catalogue record for this book is available from the British Library.

ISBN 978 1 849 90477 3

Editorial director: Albert DePetrillo
Editorial manager: Nicholas Payne
Series consultant: Justin Richards
Project editor: Steve Tribe
Proofreader: Kari Speers
Cover design: Lee Binding © Woodlands Books Ltd 2012
Cover illustration: Chris Achilleos
Production: Rebecca Jones

Printed and bound in Great Britain by Clays Ltd, St Ives PLC

Contents

INTRODUCTION
BY
Mark Gatiss

Time travel is real.

There, I've said it. I make no claims, however, for cooking up something with mirrors and static electricity, achieving faster-than-light speed or even for having ironed out those annoying teething problems with the Zigma experiments. Nevertheless, what you hold in your hands is a time machine. A Target *Doctor Who* book!

Show a copy of any one of these glorious novelisations to people of a certain age and they are transported back to a simpler, cosier age. Some of my memories of them are imprinted with Proustian clarity, like my very own, Time Lord-flavoured Madeleine cakes. *The Three Doctors* (white spine) read as I lay tucked up in Dad's Hillman Minx in the car park of Strike's Garden Centre. Watching *Chitty Chitty Bang Bang* the Saturday night Mam came back from a shopping trip to Leeds, bearing *The Auton Invasion* (brown spine) in her mittened hand. The genuinely unsettling, hard-edged face of the First Doctor gazing out from the cover of *Doctor Who and the Daleks* (purple spine) in Binns, Darlington. It became a wonderful ritual, saving pocket money, then deciding which Target book to go for. I devoured them. Not literally. Though I did live in the north and was always hungry.

Faithful to the show they certainly were, but there were things the books – being books – could do better. After all, a typewriter can take you anywhere in the universe, not just to a Home Counties quarry. Doomed minor characters were brought out and developed. Alien races developed intriguing back-stories ('They became aware of the lack of love and feeling in their lives and substituted another goal – power!'). Then there was the joy of the house style. The multitude of chapters headed 'Escape to Danger'. The classic description of the TARDIS materialising with a 'wheezing, groaning sound'. The wonderful stock descriptions of the Doctor himselves. Hartnell was usually in the 'crotchety old man in a frock coat with long flowing white hair' area, whilst Troughton had 'baggy check trousers and a mop of untidy black hair' with 'a faraway look in his eyes', which were either green/blue or blue/green and which were 'funny and sad at the same time'. My Doctor, Jon Pertwee, had an 'old/young face', a 'beak' of a nose and 'a mane of prematurely white hair', while the new (!) Doctor, the great Tom Baker, routinely had a 'mop of curly hair', a 'broad-brimmed hat' and a 'long, multi-coloured' scarf which always contributed to a 'casual bohemian elegance'.

Perhaps my fondest memory, though, is my encounter with the book you're now holding. I had already revelled in the majesty of *The Abominable Snowmen* (blue spine) and completely fallen for the Second Doctor's impish charms. The snowy wastes of Tibet had taken an immediate, Yeti-like grip on my imagination and now here was another icy adventure. As icy, indeed, as it was possible to get. *The Ice Warriors!* Featuring Viking-like Martian reptiles described elsewhere as 'a once-proud race', they instantly became one of my favourite monsters. I'd seen them, of course, on TV in glorious colour in the two Peladon stories, but here was their first, long-ago adventure. What absolutely fired my imagination as a child was the wonderful, wild world of possibilities Brian Hayles's story suggested. A distant (but not impossibly distant) future in which Mankind's meddling had plunged the Earth into another ice age. The south east of England choked by glaciers and roamed by scavenging wolves and bears. And, within it all, a base housed in a Georgian mansion where a team of hard-pressed scientists attempt to stop the remorseless advance of the glaciers. It's also an extremely prescient story, anticipating something of our current anxiety about global warming and with each side of the debate neatly characterised. The coldly logical scientists with their misplaced faith in technology and the less conventional voices who mistrust change and prefer to remain on the outside of society. It's no wonder that Troughton's scruffy, gorgeous, self-deprecating Doctor is immediately mistaken for a scavenger and threatened with transportation to Africa!

All the elements are here for a classic *Doctor Who* story, even though the idea of such a thing was really just being formed. An isolated base, a ticking clock, an unknown menace threatening life on Earth. But it's the idea of the Ice Warriors themselves that really stands the test of time. With their hissing, asthmatic speech and vaguely Nordic names, they're fierce and warlike but with strong codes of honour. The sort of alien Mars deserves. Although it is, quite rightly, the immortal Terrance Dicks who wears the Target laurels, Brian Hayles's writing here is terrific. Simple, clear and never patronising, he's also capable of as perfect, spooky and moving a moment of exposition as this: *'Suddenly, one year…' Clent paused, still remembering the terrible event, '… there was no Spring.'*

We never got to see Hayles's mooted sequel, the marvellously named 'Lords of the Red Planet', but the Martians did return to menace the Doctor and, in so doing, deservedly cemented their place at the top table of *Doctor Who* monsters. A *still*–proud race, you might say. And, surely, somewhere out there in the freezing, snowy wastes, the Ice Warriors are still waiting…

The Changing Face of Doctor Who

The Second Doctor

This *Doctor Who* novel features the second incarnation of the Doctor. After his first encounter with the Cybermen, the Doctor changed form. His old body was apparently worn out, and so he replaced it with a new, younger one. The scratchy, arrogant old man that had been the First Doctor was replaced with a younger and apparently far softer character. The First Doctor's cold, analytical abilities give way to apparent bluster and a tendency to panic under pressure.

But with the Second Doctor more than any other, first impressions are misleading. The Doctor's apparent bluster and ineptitude masks a deeper, darker nature. But there are moments too when the Second Doctor's humanity also shines through. There is ultimately no doubt that his raison d'être is to fight the evil in the universe.

Jamie

James Robert McCrimmon is the son of Donald McCrimmon, and a piper like his father and his father's father. Coming from 1746, Jamie is simple and straightforward, but he is also intelligent and blessed with a good deal of common sense. Almost everything is new to him, and while he struggles to understand he also enjoys the experience. Jamie is also extremely brave, never one to shirk a fight or run away.

Ultimately, Jamie sees the Doctor as a friend as well as a mentor. While he relishes the chance to travel and learn and have adventures, he also believes that the Doctor really does need his help.

Victoria

Victoria Waterfield is a reluctant adventurer. She travels with the Doctor through necessity rather than choice after her father was exterminated by the Daleks, leaving her stranded on Skaro. Until she was kidnapped by the Daleks, Victoria had led a sheltered and unsophisticated life. But she is clever and intelligent.

Despite the fact that both tease her at every opportunity, Victoria cares deeply for the Doctor and Jamie. But while she enjoys her time in their company, she still misses her father. She remains forever an unwilling adventurer.

1

Battle against the Glaciers

'*Stand by all personnel! Base evacuation procedure, phase one. Section leaders report immediately!*'

The urgent, metallic voice of the computer cut across the quiet bustle of the Brittanicus Base Ioniser Operations Unit. Although the monitoring technicians continued to work at their places on the central control desk, the stand-by crews moved briskly to their assembly stations, ready for routine evacuation drill.

'*Base evacuation procedure, phase one, general alert.*' Senior Control Technician Jan Garrett hurried to the sleek control deck of ECCO, the computer's communications unit, and stabbed the 'personal response' button. The streamlined, artificial head containing ECCO's video-eye swung into line with Jan's tense face.

'Reference stand-by alert,' she said tersely, cold, grey eyes frowning behind her prim spectacles. 'Explain.'

'*Threat of possible Ioniser breakdown,*' it replied crisply, without a trace of emotion. '*Relay checks report malfunction build-up. Full data not yet available. All untraced Ioniser faults require evacuation stand-by...*' it continued.

As the voice clattered on, Jan Garrett hurried in the direction of the Ioniser Control room. She didn't need a lecture from ECCO – she was all too well aware of the dangers. If the Ioniser ever got completely out of control, it would mean total disaster. Not only would the entire unit be wiped out, but this area of southern Brittanicus would be plunged into a state of radiation half-life for the next five hundred years. And without the defensive barrier of the Ioniser's heat shield, the whole island would eventually become uninhabitable, locked in the grip of a new Ice Age. But the computer, as ever, had given timely warning of trouble ahead. With ECCO to guide them, they could not fail to hold their own.

The flat voice suddenly changed in tone, rising a pitch to a higher degree of quiet alarm. '*Phase Two, amber alert. Phase Two, amber alert. All unauthorised personnel to be located and documented for departure.*'

Jan fought her way through the orderly turmoil of the Grand Hall, and entered what had once been the library of the Georgian mansion that now housed the Brittanicus Base Unit. It was in this elegant room, its paintings and its leather-bound books still preserved in their original twentieth-century state, that the compact but delicate Ioniser was housed in regal isolation, its power lines linked to the small but immensely powerful reactor unit contained in the cellars below. One glance at the machine was enough: all the tell-tale needles were sinking rapidly through amber into the red danger zones. Jan's hands began to operate the relevant controls, damping, adjusting, increasing; desperately trying to achieve stability.

Suddenly, the tension that gripped her was sharply increased by the sound of a man's voice at her shoulder. She turned. Leader Clent's face was dark with anger.

'Why has this been allowed to happen?' he snapped. 'The whole power series is barely above danger level!'

As if in response to his angry words, the needles flickered upward and held, trembling on the verge of breaking out of the amber zone. But Jan knew that the improvement could only be temporary. The flaw was basic and, as yet, its cause unknown.

'*Hold on Amber Two*,' rang out the distant warning system. '*Prepare to return to Phase One standby.*'

'That's better, Miss Garrett.' Clent's anger was now in check, and his eyes, although stern, held and calmed her. It was his strength of personality that gave backbone to this unit, many of whom had despaired of the success of a mission that had seemed doomed from the start. She was young, intelligent, well-trained; with Clent to guide her, she would eventually come to terms with the promotion he had forced upon her when the treacherous Penley...

'There was a pulse stoppage,' she blurted out, breaking his train of thoughts.

The nearly inaudible tone of the Ioniser was beginning to falter – as though the machine was sick. Clent looked grim. A pulse stoppage meant there was a danger of feedback to the reactor: the resulting explosion would wipe the Unit from the face of the Earth. But what could be causing it?

Jan's face tightened. She was close to panic.

'I'm doing all I can to boost the power impulse—'

'It can't be allowed to fall any lower!' grated Clent, studying the oscillator dials fiercely.

3

'We still have time to evacuate,' she muttered desperately.

'We will *not* evacuate!' he insisted. 'We've beaten its ridiculous tantrums before.'

As they watched, the needles began to sag ominously close to the red sector again. Miss Garrett's face grew pale with alarm. 'It's falling back again!'

'Hold it steady!' ordered Clent. 'You must!'

'I can't! It won't respond!'

Brushing Miss Garrett aside, Clent's hands moved to the controls to make the necessary adjustments.

'Then we'll switch the stabilising circuits to computer control.'

Jan watched helplessly as Clent fought to retain control of the machine.

'It's still not holding…' she whispered.

Clent was not giving up that easily. 'All circuits, woman – *all* circuits! Don't you understand?'

He snapped home a sequence of switches. Miss Garrett flashed a look of despair towards the dials showing the energy flow from the reactor. The readings were jumping wildly. She clutched Clent's arm.

'The feed-back…'

'Not enough power for that…' clipped the Leader. The scale readings were slowing at last. Clent smiled triumphantly. 'Still just outside the danger zone. We should be able to hold it there…'

He turned to Miss Garrett for agreement. She shook her head without speaking. They both knew the bitter truth. In a matter of days – hours even – the Ioniser would

4

be in a state of crisis again. But Leader Clent refused to admit defeat.

'Well at least it gives us time!' he insisted irritably, then moved to return to his personal office. He stopped, as if remembering something, and turned back. 'And while you've got the chance, call in Arden – I want him back at Base immediately!'

A geological map of the island which had once been called Britain covered one wall of the Grand Hall of Brittanicus Base. The line of electronic pin-point markers which divided the island horizontally in two seemed, at first glance, to be motionless; but they were in fact moving very slowly from north to south. Each pin-point of light represented a seismic probe set into the face of the river of ice that was threatening to engulf the island.

Brittanicus Base, the last, hastily-organised outpost of defence against the New Ice Age, was plotting the movement of the glaciers which, minute by minute, threatened to engulf it...

But the sophisticated wall chart could not reveal the bitter Polar conditions that existed outside the Base on the Cotswold hills.

Those hills and valleys which had remained free of the ice were now unrecognisable beneath their thick mantle of windswept snow. At its best the Ioniser defence could only hold back the ice; any attempt to reduce the snowy wastes would have meant disastrous flooding of the southern lowlands.

The weird landscape – a nightmare of snow and ice

which had been driven, part-melted, and had then re-frozen into bizarre grottoes and sculpted caverns – looked as bleak and unwelcoming as the wildest reaches of the Antarctic. It was impossible to imagine that this ice desert had once been green fields and gently rolling hills. Even the Scavengers – those grimly determined natives who had refused to emigrate to the more temperate climate of the equator – had fled from the hills and set up their shanty-town communes in the lowlands bordering the south coast. Only occasional fanatics determined to die amidst the snow rather than retreat, and scientists dedicated to the last-ditch Ioniser programme, could still be found on these snowswept ridges and escarpments. And no one travelled alone. Who would willingly run the risk of falling victim to wolves or polar bears?

But there were always jobs to be done, and Arden – once a keen archaeologist, and now the Base's geologist – had a particularly important one at present: that of replacing a faulty seismic probe in the ice.

The weather conditions – fine and clear – had favoured the expedition so far. But now Arden was wondering, as he glanced up towards the towering glacier face, where it would be safe to insert the pencil-slim seismic probe. The first attempt had resulted in a massive section of the ice face fracturing and falling away. But it had revealed an ideal spot for a probe: a smooth face in a relatively sheltered position, and one which allowed easy access for the sled which carried the equipment. Arden turned his goggled and hooded face towards his two companions, Walters and Davis, and beckoned them to him.

'Walters,' he shouted against the low whine of the wind, 'drill here!'

Walters, the armed member of the party, helped Davis, the seismology technician, to bring his drilling gear to the site indicated by Arden, who was already unwrapping and checking the slim seismic probe. While Davis assembled his pistol-shaped drill and connected it to the portable power pack, Walters moved to Arden's side. With a nod of his head, Arden indicated the area he had chosen.

'Clear away any loose ice, will you, Walters?' he asked.

'Sir,' acknowledged the burly security sergeant, then turned towards the ice face, and began to clear it in preparation for the drilling. Suddenly, he turned round.

'Mr Arden, sir, come quick!'

Arden hurried forward. Walters was desperately rubbing the already smooth surface of the ice with his heavy glove.

'I'll swear there's something inside the ice, sir. Look!'

Arden's passionate interest in archaeological 'finds' was known to everyone at the Base, and he wondered whether Walters was pulling his leg. He peered into the depths of the ice – and blinked! Something *was* there – and it looked like a man! Arden raised his snow goggles, and looked again, his face alive with excitement.

'What is it, sir?' asked Davis, pressing forward.

'It's… human. No, I can't be certain—' Arden spoke impatiently. 'Bring me the power light, man. Quickly!'

Davis hurriedly made the necessary connections, and shone the beam deep into the ice. What they now saw, deeply embedded and eerily green-tinted, left them dumbstruck: a massive form, possibly eight feet in height, and clad in what looked like armour – certainly its mighty head was shaped like the helmet of an ancient warrior.

Walters glanced eagerly at Arden. 'Is it a find, sir?'

'We're going to find out! Davis – the heavy drill! We'll have to start by—'

His plans were interrupted by a shrill signal from the video-communicator strapped to his wrist. He snapped it open impatiently. Atmospheric conditions were so bad that sound and picture were incomprehensible. He squinted at it for a moment – and then gave up.

'Base can wait,' he said impatiently. 'This is more important than some routine message…'

'What're we going to do then, sir?' asked Walters.

'Excavate,' replied Arden. 'This could be the find of the century!'

Keen though he was to share Arden's excitement, Walters was still a basically cautious man. 'What about our schedule, Mr Arden? We must stick to that.'

'Must we? Just because Base computer says so?'

Walters continued to look uncertain. 'Leader Clent will be furious, sir.'

'Damn the computer' – Arden grinned boyishly – '*and* Leader Clent! For once let's do something on our own account, eh?'

Walters grinned back at him.

'Can't see what Base can do about it, sir. The way things are, we can't ask permission – and they can't tell us not to, can they?'

'That's what I like to hear, Walters!' Arden slapped Walters on the shoulder, and then moved towards Davis, who was bringing the heavy drill to bear on the ice face. 'Come on, Davis, I'll give you a line to work on—'

The geologist quickly gouged a simple, coffin-shaped outline of approximately the size and shape of the mighty form within the glacier. He turned to Davis. The technician was looking at him with an uncertain expression.

'Don't worry, Davis—' Arden said firmly. 'I'll take the responsibility before Leader Clent.'

'It isn't him I'm worried about, sir,' answered Davis. He glanced upwards at the massive ridge of snow towering above them. 'There's going to be a lot of vibration, you see...'

'We'll keep an eye on that. Anyway, we have to take that chance. Now hurry, man, hurry!'

In the Grand Hall, the stand-by units were still on Phase One alert. Leader Clent, in a typical move to establish order and confidence, had called a snap inspection of the Control Area. Accompanied by Miss Garrett, he strode calmly along the line of technical operators and recited their functions.

'Emergency evacuation phasing? ... Yes. Ioniser stage fault check? Good. Reactor safety sequence in operation? Excellent.' He turned to face Miss Garrett with a confident smile that embraced all her staff. 'First class, Miss Garrett. You're to be congratulated – and, of course, your technicians, too.'

He then moved across to the computer communications deck, drawing Miss Garrett with him. As he drew alongside he murmured a dry aside. 'You'll make a qualified First Class Technical Organiser yet, Miss Garrett...'

'Thank you,' she replied with a tired smile, adding firmly, 'but we need Scientist Penley.'

Clent didn't alter his expression or even look in Jan's direction – but his voice took on an edge of cold steel.

'That person is no longer a member of this Base…' He looked sharply at Jan, his eyes chilly and commanding. 'I look to *you* to ensure that the Ioniser works properly, because *you* are loyal. Am I correct?'

The look in his eyes dared her to disagree.

'Yes, Leader Clent,' she nodded, the moment of uncertainty gone. 'You are an example to us all.'

Clent relaxed and, nodding his acknowledgement of Jan's polite submission, brought ECCO to life with a brisk tap of his finger.

'What is the latest report from the Intercontinental Ioniser Programme HQ?'

ECCO's sleek head revolved to face its questioner, and answered flatly: '*All bases on phase interlock. America – glaciers held. Australasia – glaciers held. South Africa – glaciers held. USSR – some improvement claimed…*'

Clent pulled a face, and flicked a politely amused look at Jan, who didn't respond. 'They *would* be better than the rest of us,' he muttered. His face changed as ECCO continued coldly.

'*Brittanicus Base, Europe – slipping out of phase. Glacial advance imminent unless condition stabilised immediately—*'

Clent cut the voice short. His face tightened angrily. 'Nonsense!' he snapped. 'We're holding our own! Can't they read the seismic print-outs?'

'It isn't the seismograph programme that's at fault,' Jan

replied sharply. 'It's the Ioniser. We *are* still on a Phase One alert, remember!'

'My dear Miss Garrett, that is being taken care of by the computer.'

Clent's words were lost beneath the jagged urgency of the computer public address system. Without waiting for the message to end, Clent and Jan made straight for the Ioniser Room.

'*Emergency, emergency – Phase Two, Amber Alert! Amber Alert! Emergency, emergency!*'

Clent reached the Ioniser controls first – Jan read the disaster signs from a distance. Every monitor was flickering on the verge of red – the next step, bar a miracle, would be total breakdown. Clent switched the controls over to manual, and began fighting to raise the power levels even fractionally from danger. Jan stared in despair at the elegant machine.

'We've failed,' she whispered.

'We will *not* fail!' clipped out Leader Clent. 'The glaciers haven't beaten us yet!'

'What more can we do? Inside two hours, the Ioniser will be useless! The whole European programme of glacier containment will be in ruins!'

'Not while I'm in command!' Clent, eyes fixed on the flickering needles, was adjusting the controls like a madman.

'The glaciers will start to move again,' she murmured sadly, glancing towards the electronic map. 'Five thousand years of history crushed beneath a moving mountain of ice...'

11

'Not yet, Miss Garrett. We're not finished yet!' Clent exclaimed triumphantly.

She glanced at the improved readings, and breathed a sigh of relief. But how long would it last? Clent indicated that she should take over the controls. In the near distance, the computer warning chimed on.

'*Phase Two, amber alert! All unauthorised personnel prepare to evacuate!*'

Clent punched a communication switch and spoke firmly:

'Personnel Control – advance that evacuation order. I want all unnecessary people cleared from Base. Only the emergency skeleton staff to remain. All senior grade scientists to report to me in control. Effect immediately!'

His determination had infected Jan, and she didn't hesitate to speak her mind.

'Penley could handle this. We need experts like him—'

'Don't talk to me about experts and their crazy ideas!' He paused, frowning. 'Where's Arden?'

'He's still at the ice face – completing the instrumentation project…'

'Hasn't he been warned?' demanded Clent in alarm. 'I gave you explicit instructions—'

'I couldn't get through. Conditions on the ice face made video contact impossible.'

'Miss Garrett,' snapped Clent, 'you have an unhappy habit of giving up, haven't you? I need Arden – here! Trained men are vital to our survival!'

The computer warning system had changed pitch, and

carried a new urgency. '*Emergency, Phase Two evacuation. Key personnel only to remain. Red alert to follow!*'

Clent switched the communicator to UHF frequency. 'Leader Clent to Scientist Arden. Come in, Arden! For heaven's sakes, man – answer!'

The videoscreen that should have carried Arden's image was blank. Clent repeated his call – but quickly realised it was hopeless. He moved quickly back to Miss Garrett's side.

'Hold it whatever you do,' Clent insisted harshly.

'It's slipping again. I can just about hold it by keeping it on manual... but the time interval between pulse loss is decreasing.' She looked at Clent calmly, almost resigned. 'It's not far from total disintegration...'

'Hold on, Miss Garrett,' commanded Clent quietly, 'hold on. And try everything you know!'

It was the closest thing to a prayer that Clent could manage.

The battered blue box lay toppled on its side, half-buried in a snowdrift. Seconds previously, the snow had been disturbed only by the keen sifting of the wind; then, to the accompaniment of a strange groaning rattle, the blue box had slowly materialised from a vaguely transparent shadow into solid blue reality. What would normally have been its door was now its lid. The lid opened, and from the box popped the head of what looked like a dazed jack-in-the-box. With its puckish features, tousled hair and bright-as-button eyes, it gazed at the snowy world outside in mild amazement. Soon it was joined by two companion heads

– that of a rugged-faced lad and, at his shoulder, a pretty, doll-like girl.

'Y're no flying a boat, are ye, Doctor?' The young Scot smiled at the older man. His companion looked pained.

'It was a blind landing, Jamie,' he replied apologetically.

'Aye, that's for sure!' exclaimed Jamie, starting to clamber out and offering a strong arm to the others. The girl was obviously delighted by the sight of the untrampled snow.

'There's no harm done,' she cried gaily. 'And just look at the snow…!'

'Thank you, Victoria,' said the Doctor with dignity. 'It's good to know that someone still has faith in me.'

'Snow again,' groaned Jamie in mock-disgust. 'Tibet was bad enough. Y've not landed us farther down the same mountain, have ye?'

The Doctor, having closed the door of the police box, and placed a somewhat battered, tall-crowned hat on his head, looked thoughtfully around. He shook his head.

'No, Jamie my lad – this isn't a mountain,' he mumbled, grabbing at his hat as he ducked out of the way of the snowball which had been thrown at him by Victoria. He began to gaze at what looked like a wall of ice which reared up only a foot away from the blue box. 'It's something altogether more peculiar than that.'

Intrigued by his voice, and puzzled by the curious way in which he was sweeping the snow from the ice face, the two youngsters scrambled to join him. Victoria stared at the smooth, dull grey substance that he had uncovered, then looked at the Doctor with laughing, rounded eyes.

'It looks like a great wall of ice,' she exclaimed. 'Perhaps

14

it's the Palace of the Snow Queen!'

'It's not ice, Victoria,' commented the Doctor, 'it's plastic.'

Jamie put his hand on the material, then nodded. 'Aye,' he agreed, 'it's no really cold. But it's so smooth and curved, can ye no see?'

The Doctor took a pace or two backwards, nearly falling as he did so. 'It's a dome,' he declared. 'Some sort of protective dome…'

'But it must be huge,' Victoria wondered aloud. 'I can't see any end to it, can you?' She turned to the Doctor eagerly. 'I wonder what's inside!'

'There's no door,' observed Jamie with dour Scots realism. No sooner had he spoken than the quiet hum of electrically operated machinery reached their ears. The youngsters, reacting quickly to the Doctor's warning gesture, huddled down behind a drift of snow. Now they could see without being seen…

A door in the plastic surface beneath the ice slid back, and two ragged, unkempt figures stepped out. Having glanced furtively to left and right, the smaller of the two dropped several of the parcels he was carrying; his companion, burlier, and with a wild shaggy beard that made him look like a pirate, snapped at him irritably.

'What're you doing? Come on, man, hurry!'

The smaller man hurriedly picked up what he'd dropped, and stowed away his obviously precious prizes in a number of the many pockets which seemed to be concealed beneath his layers of protective animal skin. He seemed much calmer than his irritable comrade.

'Don't worry. That alarm wasn't because of us.' He started off again, his ill-gotten goods tucked safely away in his poacher's pockets – then paused, and looked back thoughtfully. 'I wonder what's wrong, though…'

'That's their problem,' growled the bearded scavenger. 'Come on, let's get away from here!'

For all his bulk, the big man moved through the snow as swiftly as a hunter. The little poacher followed him energetically but with less skill, floundering through the drifts as though unused to legwork. Soon, both men were out of sight. The Doctor and his companions emerged from behind the snowdrift and hurried eagerly towards the sliding door. It fitted perfectly, and seemed to be without handles or catches. It seemed impossible to open – until the Doctor found a pressure control in the plastic moulding which surrounded the entrance. He pressed it. With a gentle whine of power, the door panel slid back. A small vestibule faced them – with an identical door beyond. Jamie saw the opening device there, strode forward, and pressed it – but it wouldn't budge. He turned back to the Doctor, and shrugged helplessly.

'It's locked.'

'For a very simple reason, Jamie.' Seeing the exasperation on Jamie's face, the Doctor quickly supplied his explanation. 'It's an airlock. It won't open until we've closed the outer door.'

'But why?' asked Victoria. 'There's nothing wrong with the air outside, is there? We were able to breathe all right.'

The Doctor smiled, and ushered Victoria into the airlock before shutting out the world of snow. 'If my guess is right,' he said, 'I think we're in for a pleasant surprise...' He pressed the button. The inner door slid back to reveal a scene that made even the Doctor wonder. There, under an immense plastic dome that kept the Arctic weather conditions at bay, stood a gracious and elegant Georgian country house in a state of perfect preservation. Ahead of them, across a short stretch of lawn, a terrace and a side door opened into the stable block. The Doctor's eyes twinkled with appreciation. 'Absolutely charming,' he said, with a smile. 'Shall we go in?'

2

Two Minutes to Doomsday

Clent stood before the electronic chart that dominated the Grand Hall of the Base HQ. Beads of perspiration broke out on his forehead as he watched the line that represented the glacier flow minutely forward... With the Ioniser now operating at less than half power, the ice could barely be held in check. And if it failed completely, there would be nothing to stop the glaciers' advance to the Channel, and beyond. What is more, his own career would be in ruins.

'Leader Clent!'

Miss Garrett was hurrying towards him, her face alert and, for once, pleased.

'We've made contact with Scientist Arden!' she announced.

Clent strode to the nearest video point, and Miss Garrett channelled the call through to him. In spite of interference and atmospherics, Arden's goggled face was plainly visible.

'Arden' – the Leader ordered firmly – 'you must return to Base immediately!'

'Sorry, Clent,' replied the geologist, 'but we haven't finished yet. Another hour, and then we'll be back.'

'Now!' insisted Clent. 'The Ioniser is close to breakdown – you know what that means!'

'Chilly weather ahead,' joked the grinning face on the interference-flecked videoscreen. 'I wonder if Penley's ears are burning?'

Stung into anger, Clent barked out his reply. 'I'm giving you an order, Arden. You'll return now – and no arguments!'

'I've got good reason to delay,' replied Arden without flinching. 'A fantastic discovery in the ice—'

'Your task was to replace a probe!' Clent's anger boiled over. 'You are not there to indulge in amateur archaeology! Do you hear?'

Arden was unimpressed. 'Even when the discovery is a man?'

Jan, standing at Clent's shoulder, could see he was surprised, even impressed, but his reply was typically crushing.

'Congratulations – it makes a change from pottery fragments! Now leave it and return – as ordered!'

'As soon as I've got the body loaded on to the airsled,' commented the grinning geologist. 'I'm bringing it back with me, Clent. These blasted glaciers owe me that much!'

Clent fumed. He was helpless – and Arden knew it.

'There will be a full disciplinary enquiry!' he snapped.

'Can't hear you, old chap… too much interference… see you shortly.'

The screen went blank.

At the same moment, the computer warning system went into Phase Three – Red Alert.

*

The door from the stable courtyard led directly into a passageway connecting the servants' kitchens with the main body of the house. There was no sign of life as yet – except the distant repetition of the warning relay. Leading the way, the Doctor paused at the heavy door. He placed his ear against it, and listened intently. Victoria was gazing round, wondering whether she was in a dream – the house so much resembled the Victorian mansion that had once been her home!

'It's a lovely old house,' she sighed. Jamie, like the Doctor, was more concerned with the possible dangers ahead.

'What's that they're saying, Doctor…?' he queried.

The Doctor could only frown and shake his head. He opened the door a fraction, so that the warning voice could be heard more clearly.

'Phase Three. Red alert. Evacuate. Evacuate. Transport section leaders report to loading bays. Phase Three. Evacuate!'

'There's something wrong…' the Doctor murmured.

'It looks peaceful enough to me,' commented Victoria.

'Come on. Let's see if we can find out.' The Doctor opened the door into the broad main corridor beyond. For a brief moment, they stood alone in the deserted corridor; then, as though summoned by a bugle call, a small group of grimly determined men erupted from a corner passageway and charged straight at the Doctor and his young friends. With no possible chance to run or hide, they stood resigned to being captured – the Doctor even going so far as to raise his arms above his head in surrender.

To their astonishment, the task force ran straight past them, down the corridor, and disappeared out of sight.

Almost disappointed, the Doctor called after them half-heartedly, 'I say, could you tell me the way to...' His voice trailed off, and meeting the puzzled faces of his young companions, he shrugged. 'It's all very strange...'

Another man ran up from the opposite direction, but, like the previous party, his face looked determined and set. The Doctor smiled and tried to catch the runner's eye. He stretched out his hand. 'Excuse me, old chap—'

The only response was a shove in the chest as the runner dashed past, that sent the Doctor staggering into Jamie's arms. Victoria could only stand and giggle as the Doctor, a look of bewilderment on his face, set his hat straight.

'They don't seem to think much of you, Doctor...'

'I can't understand it,' muttered the Doctor. An attractive girl now walked up to them and, without uttering a word, briskly attached numbered plastic tags to their lapels. She had finished the job and moved on before Jamie had recovered sufficiently from his surprise to call out to her – but she paid no attention.

The Doctor smiled. 'She doesn't want to know, Jamie...'

Victoria had twisted her tag so that she could read it.

'It says we're on Evacuation Flight Seven!'

'Not very hospitable, is it,' commented the Doctor. 'We've only just arrived.'

'Hey, and have ye seen *this*!' Jamie showed them the reverse side of his tag. 'It says we're scavengers! I'll not have that – I'm no beggar!'

Victoria couldn't help laughing at the insult to his Scots dignity, but the Doctor had moved to a nearby doorway and was listening intently to a faint sound coming from within.

'Shush a minute, Jamie lad,' said the Doctor.

At that moment, the relayed warning call drowned the sound from beyond the door as it repeated its ominous broadcast.

'Phase Three, red alert. Evacuate immediately. Flights One to Five now on departure circuit. Flights Six and Seven, stand by. Phase Three, red alert...'

When the warning had ceased, the Doctor beckoned Jamie and Victoria back to the door. They could hear vague humming – but nothing they could identify.

'What is it, Doctor?' asked Victoria, intrigued.

The Doctor looked thoughtful, and not a little worried. 'I'd say it's electronic machinery of some kind – perhaps a computer – but there's something badly wrong with its pitch...'

'It's no ours – let's leave it', suggested Jamie. He knew all too well from past experience where the Doctor's curiosity could lead them – usually into trouble. Victoria agreed.

'It could be dangerous,' she pointed out.

But the Doctor had already made up his mind, and quietly opened the door. 'Stay out here if you like,' he murmured, 'but I'm going in.'

In the Ioniser Room, the tension was electric. Jan Garrett was standing poised over the main control deck; Clent strode nervously from monitor to monitor, noting the figures presented by each. At the door leading into the Grand Hall, stood two security guards, their backs to the library interior. Because of this, the Doctor –

23

followed reluctantly by Jamie and Victoria – was able to enter unnoticed. While they paused to take in the bizarre contrast of the ultra-modern electronic gadgetry and the antique library setting, the Doctor moved stealthily behind Clent, and began to jot down the monitor readings on his shirt cuff. His face grew more and more disturbed.

'Still out of phase...' muttered Clent, unaware of the bizarre onlooker at his shoulder. 'Seven two point four...'

'Seven two point four?' repeated the Doctor to himself. 'That's bad...'

'We must balance those readings, Miss Garrett!' declared the Leader. 'Seventeen degrees off the norm!'

Jan heard, but could do little; her eyes remained glued to the control panel.

Clent paused anxiously before the final monitor screen; he mopped his brow with his handkerchief and whispered the desperate figures to himself.

'One three seven nine already... If it reaches fifteen hundred...' He took a deep breath. How long could they last?

'One three seven nine!' echoed the Doctor, his face expressing equal alarm. Unable to keep quiet any longer, he tapped Clent on the shoulder. Jamie and Victoria held their breath. What was he doing?

'Excuse me,' said the Doctor politely, 'but I'm afraid you're in serious trouble here, old chap...'

Clent turned on the Doctor. The sight of the oddly dressed, obviously non-scientific intruder brought a flush of justifiable anger to his face.

'Who the blazes are you?' he demanded. Without

waiting for a reply, he shouted an order to the security guards. 'Get these scavengers out of here – quickly!'

'I'm trying to help!' protested the Doctor as he and his young friends were expertly bundled towards the corridor.

'Get them on to the next available flight out of here!' shouted Clent. He turned back to the control panel dismissively.

'In two minutes thirty eight seconds,' cried the Doctor, as he was pushed out of the door, 'that Ioniser is going to explode. The readings say so. Why don't you do something about it?' The effect on Garrett and the guards was startling; even Clent froze in shocked alarm.

'You can't possibly know that!' he snapped. 'I haven't even processed the figures through the computer yet!'

'My dear chap, I don't need a computer!' replied the Doctor.

For once, Clent paused, unsure of himself. Garrett flung a look of grim desperation at her leader.

'If he's right, it's already too late to escape,' she stated icily. The security men, uncertain what to do, made no attempt to check the Doctor as he slipped quickly back into the room.

'It doesn't *have* to happen. If you'll just allow me…' he said brightly, his hands already hovering over the controls.

'Don't!' shouted Clent. But his cry came too late. The Doctor had gone into immediate action – and as though mesmerised by the stranger's personality, Miss Garrett was actually helping him!

'Uncouple the stabilising circuits and the reactor link for a start,' the Doctor directed, his eyes taking in the monitor readings. Jan obeyed automatically.

'Raise the density phasing to par… quick as you can!'

Miss Garrett frowned. 'There isn't enough power—'

'Then we'd better produce some, hadn't we? A short burst from the reactor link – now!'

Without arguing, Jan switched on a heavy duty connector; there was an immediate hum of power.

'Now off!' commanded the Doctor. Then, without waiting for her to complete the action, he snapped home a series of switches. 'Tie in each of the circuits to the reactor link… *now* bring in the computer stabiliser…' He paused, then smiled to himself, obviously pleased. 'That should hold it, I think…'

He turned. Clent and Miss Garrett were looking at him in sheer amazement. That a ragged clown could perform such a miracle! Remembering his earlier brusqueness, the Doctor began to apologise.

'Not a perfect job, mind you…' he murmured genially. 'You ought to get an expert in really…'

Clent, remembering his position as Leader of the Base, snapped out of his reverie and tried to reassert his authority.

'It was all bluff, wasn't it – that business about two minutes thirty-eight seconds to destruction?'

The Doctor looked modestly pained, but spoke quietly.

'Not in the least. It was near enough correct – give or take a second or two.'

'Rubbish!' snapped Clent, irritated by the thought that a human being could be the equal of his beloved computer.

The Doctor looked offended and angry.

'Check it on your precious computer then – go on!'

Clent stared at him, then smiled arrogantly.

'Miss Garrett,' he ordered, 'process those figures, please.'

Jan activated ECCO and read out the relevant figures, while Clent hovered over her, smiling smugly.

'Ioniser fall rate – seven two point four... Ion compensator – minus seventeen degrees... Ion flow rate – one three seven nine. Assessment, please.'

The computer's reply was virtually immediate. As it spoke, the smirk was wiped from Clent's face, and he stared at the Doctor with something akin to respect.

'*Immediate emergency!*' announced the computer. '*In two minutes thirty-seven seconds, the reactor will suffer feed-back and explode! Action must be taken—*'

Miss Garrett ended its panic, and looked towards Clent. It was a long time since she had seen him accept another scientist as his equal. Would he reject this one, as he had rejected Penley and so many others before him?

'I apologise for the odd second,' muttered the Doctor modestly. 'But we can't all be perfect, can we...'

'Leader Clent,' interjected Jan, barely restraining her excitement, 'it's steady on half power now. We can hold our own!'

Its oscillators steady, the machine's operating purr was soft as silk – the healthiest it had been for weeks. This stranger certainly knew what he was up to... Clent frowned.

'Even Penley couldn't have done better,' he admitted. 'But where on earth have you sprung from?'

27

The Doctor threw a sharp look back at Jamie and Victoria, and raised his eyebrows. Then he turned back to Clent, smiled and shrugged his shoulders. He didn't want to have to enter into a full explanation – and fortunately Clent was in no mood for it. In spite of being desperately tired, he was elated. Perhaps they could still win! He clapped the Doctor on the shoulder, and then read the details on his plastic tag. His mind was made up.

'Flight Seven, eh?' he repeated. 'There won't be any need for that. Come with me to the laboratory – I think there's something we need to discuss…'

At last the great block of ice stood free from the glacier face! Arden gazed in excitement; even Walters and Davis were impressed. And within it: the massive figure of an armoured man, which looked like a monument to some ancient king…

'Amazing…' whispered Walters.

'A giant among prehistoric men,' agreed Arden, his mind racing. This discovery must go back at least three thousand years!

'Is it a sort of armour he's got on, sir?' asked Davis.

'Yes,' replied Arden. 'And that's the most exciting thing about it. You see, he looks pre-Viking… but no such civilisation existed in the prehistoric period before the first Ice Age.'

'Proper sort of ice warrior, I'd call him,' suggested Walters, smiling.

'A good description, Walters,' Arden agreed. 'Even from here you can see how cruel and terrifying he must have been…'

He recalled the old legends of the Viking raiders; brutal, bloodthirsty killers, whose only ambition had been conquest.

'I reckon even Leader Clent'll want to take a second look, don't you, sir?' asked Walters.

'I should hope so. And what do you think that blessed computer will make of it, eh?'

Davis had finished packing away his drilling equipment.

'We'd better be getting back, sir,' he said, looking up at the sky, 'while the weather holds…'

Arden nodded in agreement. Time for celebration when they'd got the Ice Warrior back to Base. What Clent would say was anybody's guess – but he couldn't deny that it was a find of great importance.

'Bring the airsled as close as possible,' Arden ordered, 'and we'll get him loaded up.'

The three men, now fully absorbed in their difficult task, were totally unaware of being observed. Less than a hundred yards away, hidden by a wind-scoured outcrop of ice, the pirate and the poacher crouched and watched intently.

'What're they up to, Penley?' asked the big man suspiciously. He smelt potential danger in anything that Clent's scientists got up to – and he didn't like the look of this particular bunch one little bit…

'I don't know, Storr old son,' cheerfully replied Penley, shrewder and more thoughtful. 'Arden must've found something buried in the ice, something to take home to Clent.' He smiled knowingly. 'It won't be appreciated though…'

Storr glowered, his wild beard making his fierce gaze look even more ferocious. 'Why don't they leave well alone?'

Penley knew all about Storr's hatred of technology. He tried to explain what he knew would be in Arden's mind – a quality he'd once admired when they'd been working colleagues.

'Arden was always a searcher. He was an archaeologist once.'

'Archaeology!' sneered the burly hunter. 'What good's that?'

'It's good to know things, Storr – even if they're dead.'

'Nothing's sacred to you blasted scientists, is it?'

'It's in my character to ask questions, I suppose. Sorry.'

'You swore you'd give all that up! Changed your mind, have you?'

Penley turned to Storr, his dirty face full of patience – and determination. 'Look, old son, discovery is as exciting and purposeful to me as hunting game is to you.' He could see that Storr wasn't convinced, and continued sarcastically, 'We're not all like Clent, you know. He's the kind that uses scientist's skulls as stepping stones to the top jobs…'

Storr smiled at this manifestation of Penley's bitterness and then changed the subject.

'Come on, we've got to move. Let's leave them to their stupid games!'

He turned away from the sight of the scientific party loading their airsled, and moved skilfully across the snow, followed by Penley. Coming to a small crevasse, he paused. Beyond it was a glacier overhang that would give them all the cover they'd need. But to get there would mean a leap across the open fissure that would bring them into full view of the scientists. Storr motioned Penley to wait, and watched for the moment when the distant trio, who were still working on the upper glacier face, were turned away from them. Suddenly he saw that something had distracted them. Pushing Penley ahead, he prepared to spring across the gap...

It was Davis who first heard the ominous rumble. He looked up, and saw a tell-tale spume of blinding snow was almost on top of him! Of the three, his position on top of the ridge of ice was the most vulnerable. He screamed a desperate warning to the other two below, then dived for cover.

'Avalanche!'

Arden simultaneously heard the cry and the terrifying roar of approaching snow and ice. He instinctively looked upwards to locate Davis – but he was hurled to the ground and dragged into the shelter of the airsled by Walters before he could catch his breath to reply.

The avalanche, sweeping diagonally across the ice face, caught up Davis and continued towards that same crevasse that Storr and Penley were on the point of crossing.

Storr thrust Penley violently forward into the protection of the overhang, and tried to hurl himself forward after him. Penley watched in horror, as the ice and snow, raging over and past him, caught Storr's arm and shoulder, and snatched him into the drifts farther down the slope.

Suddenly the avalanche had passed; all was still once more. Half afraid of what he would find, Penley staggered out from safety to look for Storr – but it was Davis he reached first. The angle of the technician's neck told him there was no hope there. Hearing a growl of pain to the left, Penley scrambled through the churned-up snow and found Storr struggling to dig himself free. His left arm hung ominously limp and twisted.

'Storr!' gasped Penley. 'Are you all right?'

'My damned arm…' groaned the hunter. 'It's broken.'

Penley strapped the shattered arm as tight as he could against Storr's body.

'You're lucky,' he gasped. 'There's one over there who'll be staying on the mountain for good.'

Storr shook Penley off, and lurched to his feet. 'Come on,' he gritted through the haze of pain, 'they'll be here any minute, looking for him. Let's get away from here!'

Penley hesitated, wondering whether Storr was capable of the effort. Storr glowered back at him, sneering bitterly.

'Unless you fancy turning me over to your friends?'

Penley met his gaze squarely and replied without hesitation. 'Six months ago, they were my friends – but not now.' Uncertain how to best help his surly companion, he stepped back and frowned. 'Can you walk…?'

'Just make sure you keep up!' grunted Storr, and strode off, calling back over his shoulder, 'Come on!'

With a last sad glance at the dead man in the snow, Penley hurried after Storr beneath the ominous shadow of the glacier.

Walters had struggled to his feet, and was now helping

Arden up. There was no sign of Davis.

'I'll go and look for him, sir,' Walters said curtly, to Arden's unspoken question. He wasn't going to waste his breath offering unnecessary hope. Arden watched him go, sensing his despair. If Davis was lost, Clent would tolerate no excuses – least of all an archaeological find. While he busied himself completing the job of lashing the block of ice to the airsled, Arden's mind raged with self-doubt: if they had ignored the Ice Warrior; if they hadn't used the heavy drill; if they'd left when Davis had indicated… Would he have still been with them? Arden wasn't a superstitious man, but he paused and stared into the ice block at the ominous, helmeted figure, and wondered…

Abruptly, he dismissed from his mind the ridiculous thought that there might have been some ancient curse attached to disturbing this ice-bound giant from his deathly sleep. But when he heard Walters' dejected call, and saw him point miserably at the snow some two hundred yards away, the chilling thought needled his mind again. Had the Ice Warrior claimed his first victim?

The laboratory had been established in the part of the house that had once been called the gun room. It was, in fact, a complex series of small rooms, each of which served a purpose related to the laboratory central unit: storerooms for expedition equipment, weapons, geological analysis; and a medicare centre that had proved invaluable to the mental and physical well-being of the Base scientists.

The tensions created by the importance of their mission, and the conflict of personalities under continuous pressure of work, had brought several of the staff near to breaking point. Only Clent had seemed impervious to strain so far.

But now he willingly relaxed in the vibro-chair. Its effect was to relax the mind and tone up the body cells. The expression on Clent's face also showed that it was extremely enjoyable into the bargain. Even so, although reclining and at ease, he lost none of his authority as Leader. If anything, the quiet hum of the electronic chair seemed to give an added keenness to the questions he threw at the Doctor who, like Jamie and Victoria, was immensely intrigued by the compact technology of the medicare unit.

'You call yourself "Doctor",' continued Clent, 'yet you have no proof of your qualifications. Why's that?'

'Aren't we wasting time?' replied the Doctor evasively. 'If you really want my help, hadn't you better explain the whole situation?'

'Explain the situation?' Clent raised his eyebrows in surprise and glanced towards Miss Garrett, who echoed his reaction. 'My dear man, where have you been all these years?'

The Doctor threw a quick look at Jamie and Victoria before replying with a nervous smile. 'As a matter of fact, we've been on a sort of… retreat – in Tibet.'

Victoria had to turn away slightly to hide the smile that threatened to flood her face.

'Oh… really?' replied Clent. 'Tibet… of course.' He looked towards Miss Garrett for her opinion – but she was gazing silently at the floor.

'Well,' continued Clent, 'as for the general situation,

Miss Garrett can give you all the details later. Before we get to that stage, I want you to take a simple test.'

'I'm not much of a one for examinations,' observed the Doctor drily.

'This is a verbal exercise in deductive logic. It'll tell me whether you're up to the standard I require. I don't tolerate charlatans, you know.'

'And if I don't come up to scratch?' enquired the Doctor.

'You'll be evacuated with the other scavengers.'

'Where to?' asked Jamie bluntly.

'To one of the African Rehabilitation Centres, of course,' replied Miss Garrett with cold formality.

'Oh, no!' objected Victoria. 'Not Africa!'

The Doctor shared her alarm. It wasn't the country that was objectionable, so much as the fact that their only means of escape from this particular time zone lay outside the Base – half-buried in a snowdrift! To be transported to Africa would mean being parted from the TARDIS – and probably for good.

'Let's hear this problem then,' the Doctor demanded quietly.

'Very well,' said Clent. 'All the major continents are threatened by destruction beneath the glaciers of the New Ice Age. How would you halt the ice surge and return the climate to normal, using the equipment you've already seen?'

The Doctor frowned, and puffed his cheeks at the enormity of the question. Both Jamie and Victoria stared at him anxiously. Smiling blandly, Clent sat up in the vibro-chair and reached out a hand to the chronometer by his side.

'You have just ninety seconds,' he murmured, 'from now!'

Victoria and Jamie could only stare at the Doctor's fiercely concentrating face, as he fired out questions and comments that left them completely baffled. Clent, relaxed, had closed his eyes; Miss Garrett studied the Doctor with sharp interest, noting with approval the scope and alertness of his mental responses. This man was certainly no charlatan!

'Possible causes, then,' rapped out the Doctor keenly. 'A reversal of the Earth's magnetic poles?'

'No such change has occurred,' replied Clent, without opening his eyes. The smile had vanished. Only a trained scientist could have asked such a question.

'Interstellar clouds obscuring the sun's rays?'

Clent shook his head.

Negative again. But the Doctor hadn't finished.

'A severe shift in the Earth's axis of rotation?'

Once more, Clent indicated that the suggestion was wrong. The Doctor looked thoughtful; he'd been given a problem without clues – the most difficult sort. And time was slipping away...

'Come on, Doctor!' urged Victoria. 'Think!'

The Doctor looked at the recumbent Clent, and a slow, wicked smile spread over his puckish features.

'Ah! A gigantic heat loss – is that it?'

The Leader's face gave nothing away. He glanced briefly at the chronometer, then again closed his eyes before replying to the question.

'I require an answer – not a question. You have rather less than thirty seconds left, Doctor.'

Clent's carefully concealed reaction wasn't lost on the Doctor. He grinned inwardly – two could play at that game!

'In that case, it's perfectly simple…' he said airily, then paused, apparently lost in an attempt to read his plastic evacuation tag upside down. By the time the chronometer's flicking hand had reached five seconds to zero, not only the youngsters and Miss Garrett were on tenterhooks, but Clent himself was sitting up in the vibro-chair and gripping its arms in expectation.

'Well?' he demanded. 'Hurry, man – speak up!'

The Doctor looked up at Clent with mild surprise – as though he'd forgotten the Leader was there. 'Ionisation,' he said precisely, as the clockhand reached zero.

'Is he right?' asked Jamie anxiously.

'Yes,' admitted Clent warily, 'he is.'

'But… ionisation?' interrupted Victoria. 'What does it mean? I don't understand.'

'It's to do with the carbon dioxide content of the Earth's atmosphere, Victoria,' explained the Doctor. 'It's only a fractional proportion, but it helps to retain the heat of the sun, after it's filtered through to the planet's surface.'

'Like a sort of invisible blanket, you mean?' Victoria was trying hard to understand.

'Something like that, yes,' beamed the Doctor. 'Now – if you take the gas away, or even unbalance its mixture too much, the sun's reflected heat is rapidly dispersed, our

37

planet cools down too quickly and we're left with the sort of freeze-up these people have now. Is that clear?'

Victoria nodded brightly. But Jamie was still puzzled.

'But where did all this carbon dioxide gas go to?' he asked. It was Clent who answered – almost apologetically.

'Our civilisation is supremely efficient, my boy – thanks to the guidance we receive from the Intercontinental Computer Complex. With its help, we conquered the problem of world famine many years ago, using artificial foods, and protein recycling. Unfortunately, the recycling process got rather out of hand…'

'I suppose you started artificial recycling of waste gases to produce more oxygen,' remarked the Doctor, frowning.

'That,' agreed Clent, 'plus a massive increase in intensive depollution processes.' He looked defensively at the Doctor. 'A minor error in atmospheric prediction…'

'But one which produced a nasty imbalance in the protective layers of the Earth's atmosphere,' added the Doctor soberly.

'Suddenly, one year…' Clent paused, still remembering the terrible event, '… there was no Spring.'

No one spoke for a moment. Then Clent continued breezily.

'The danger wasn't understood at first – not until the polar ice caps started to advance.' He smiled confidently. 'But we soon came up with the answer to that!'

'This blessed Ioniser, do you mean?' questioned Jamie.

'Precisely,' beamed Clent. But Jamie wasn't to be put off so easily.

'Precisely what, though?' he asked shrewdly. 'What does it do exactly?'

Miss Garrett cut in with an explanation. 'Ionisation is a method of intensifying the sun's heat on to the Earth – but only on selected areas.'

'Try thinking of it as a sort of burning glass, Jamie,' added the Doctor.

Jamie's face immediately brightened. 'Och, now I understand!' he cried, 'Like ye can burn paper and make fire?'

'So you can actually melt the glaciers and change the weather?' Victoria asked Clent, wide-eyed.

'When certain difficulties are overcome,' he said.

'It's a highly complex system,' stated Miss Garrett. 'The focusing process is very delicate, and there aren't enough specialists who understand its manipulation.'

'Can't afford to make mistakes, can you?' observed the Doctor. 'Might cause some nasty floods if all that ice melted too quickly.'

'There's the opposite problem, too,' admitted Clent. 'The ionisation process can produce temperatures intense enough to melt rock.'

'But your computer can't quite manage to strike the happy medium,' reasoned the Doctor – 'at least, not without the assistance of one of those specialists you're so short of…'

'One of my scientists – a chap called Penley – had some sort of a breakdown, and went missing.' Clent paused; he didn't like asking favours. 'I'd like you to take his place. It's a worthwhile mission. Will you join us?'

The Doctor caught the resigned look that passed between Jamie and Victoria – they knew what his decision would be.

'I'm willing to try,' he said modestly.

'Good!' exclaimed Clent, smiling broadly. 'Er... you have worked with computers, I presume?'

'No more than necessary,' muttered the Doctor.

'Miss Garrett is our technical expert,' Clent beamed. 'She'll help you.'

Miss Garrett was proud of her computer training, and intended the Doctor to know it. 'Our computers check every decision to eliminate the risk of failure,' she declared. 'Our standards are of the highest—'

'So I've noticed,' remarked the Doctor with a wry smile.

'Who sets these standards, though?' demanded Victoria, who had a distinct aversion to bossy machines.

Miss Garrett looked at the pretty teenager over her glasses. 'World Computer Control, of course,' she snapped.

'Another machine?' queried Jamie, amazed. 'In charge of what everybody does? Och, that's ridiculous!'

'The machine,' snapped Miss Garrett, 'is rational, coherent, and infallible!'

'But not very human,' suggested the Doctor. He turned to face Clent. 'Is that why Penley defected?'

'The pressure of work here *has* driven some men into... weakness.'

'But not you.'

Clent faced the Doctor squarely, and replied with a tense dignity.

'I have a job to do… and I do not intend to fail. My duty is to make the Ionisation programme succeed – and save five thousand years of European civilisation! I *must* not fail!'

In the pause that followed, only the Doctor saw the desperate plea in Clent's eyes. It was impossible to ignore his silent appeal for help.

'I respect that, Leader Clent,' conceded the Doctor. 'Now tell us how we can help.'

Before Clent could say what was in his mind, the double doors of the laboratory swung open, and Arden walked in. At first, Clent didn't see Walters and the other technicians wheeling the trolley behind the defiant scientist. He swung himself from the vibro-chair in a blaze of anger.

'Arden! Is this what you call co-operation?' Clent strode forward fiercely. 'How are we expected to carry out this project when idiots like you—'The Leader stopped abruptly, in full flow. Arden had stepped aside, and for the first time Clent caught sight of the prize he had brought back from the glacier. No one spoke. They were all gazing speechless at the mighty form contained within the great chunk of ice. That one moment alone was triumph enough for Arden.

'I thought you might be interested, Clent,' declared the geologist perkily. He turned to his helpers, and pointed to a corner of the room. 'Wheel him over there.'

The others followed, hardly able to take their eyes from Arden's discovery. As yet, the ice had barely started to melt.

'Doctor,' whispered Victoria, 'what is it?'

Jamie's eyes shone with admiration. 'It's a great warrior! Do ye no see his war helmet?'

The Doctor inspected the warrior thoughtfully. 'Frozen for centuries and perfectly preserved,' he said, then added, 'odd, though…'

Arden had succeeded in silencing Clent, but hadn't yet summoned up the courage to tell him of Davis's death. He now turned on the Doctor suspiciously. 'Who are you?'

Clent stepped in with an explanation. 'An addition to our staff, Arden. I'll explain at the meeting.' He turned to the Doctor, intrigued by his snap criticism. 'What exactly is it that you find odd?'

'The armour, it's all wrong. When this man was frozen to death, only primitive cavemen existed…'

Arden lunged forward and confronted the Doctor defiantly.

'Well I say it's an undiscovered civilisation! Think of the implications!'

Clent needed time to think, and a full scale discussion of Arden's find was the last thing he wanted at the moment. The geologist would have to be reprimanded – yet what he had found was obviously of sufficient importance to interest world authorities. But everything depended on the success of the Ioniser mission. First things first, then.

'Arden, whatever the implications, this find of yours must take second place to our project,' declared Clent. He watched as the young geologist connected the output leads of a portable power pack to electrode points on the horizontal block of ice. 'You can give me a full appraisal of your theories after the meeting,' he consulted his watch, 'which will commence in three minutes fifteen seconds exactly.'

Without seeming to hurry unduly, Arden had completed

his power connections and was ready to go.

'Miss Garrett, perhaps you'd lead the way?' continued Clent. 'Come along, Arden. You can play with your toy later. You'll be needed at the meeting too, Doctor.'

With that, he and his colleagues passed through the swing doors towards the conference room.

The Doctor may have heard Clent's last words – if so, he showed no inclination to obey them. Instead, alone with Jamie and Victoria, he stood hunched over the ice-encased giant, studying it intently. Jamie pointed to the wiring and the black power pack that Arden had attached to the ice.

'What's all this about, Doctor?'

'It's a portable power pack, Jamie,' the Doctor explained. 'Arden has set the current so that it will melt the ice very slowly.'

'But it's working quite quickly – look!' cried Victoria.

Jamie and the Doctor looked to where her finger was pointing, and saw that a large flake of ice had fallen away from the side of the warrior's helmet. He didn't, however, hear the faint but ominous humming which seemed to come from the power pack. The Doctor didn't notice. The Doctor bent close to the helmet, examining it through the cloak of thin ice with an expression of intense astonishment.

'But that's… incredible!' he blurted out.

'What is, Doctor?' asked Jamie in amazement. It wasn't often something set the Doctor back on his heels!

'Jamie…' murmured the Doctor wonderingly, 'that's an electronic earpiece – there, on the helmet! Almost identical to the ones used on modern space helmets!'

Both the youngsters looked at him uncomprehendingly.

'But Doctor… it can't be,' said Victoria finally.

The Doctor raised his head abruptly. His voice was keen with excitement, and possibly something more… 'Don't you realise what this means?'

He looked into their young faces, and saw that they did not understand. Reaching a quick decision, he hurried towards the door.

'Wait here,' he shouted back over his shoulder, 'and don't touch anything!'

Jamie and Victoria were getting used to his sudden exits, and exchanged a gentle chuckle.

'I wonder what sent him off like that?' asked Jamie.

'Scientists are all the same,' replied Victoria. 'They're forever shouting *Eureka*, or something. Hey! What are you doing? Don't be a spoilsport!'

Half playfully, she struggled to prise Jamie out of the vibro-chair – not because the Doctor had told them not to touch it, but because she dearly wanted to have a go in it herself. 'Me first!' she shouted, then gasped as she felt the machine tingle into life, switched on by Jamie's eager hand, as he relaxed in the chair.

Neither of them noticed that more ice had fallen away from the warrior's helmet. The power pack's electrodes were now touching bare metal. Their excited laughter hid the hum which was coming from the prostrate form, and which seemed to be ever increasing in volume.

They didn't see the eye-pieces of the cruel helmet flicker, nor the reflex twitch of the great, gauntleted hand.

Slowly but surely, the Ice Warrior was coming to life…

3

Creature from the Red Planet

The Doctor had been summoned to Clent's meeting – but he hadn't been told how to get there. Flustered and irritated, his brain almost bursting with the news of the terrible discovery, the Doctor turned a corner and found himself in the main reception hall. He paused, and took a deep breath. This sort of building must be like others of its period. If he could just mentally picture the architectural plans: music room ahead… next to that the ballroom or great hall… to the rear of the house, leading from the great hall… the library or study. The Doctor opened his eyes, his mind alert. The library – that was it!

The memory of the Ioniser control room, lined with elegant bookcases and splendid antique paintings, echoed in his mind – as did the half-remembered glimpse he had had into the vast room beyond, filled with its banks of computers and monitoring equipment. That'd be the place! Quickly, he orientated himself in line with the room plan he had formed in his head and then set off once again, grimly determined.

His latest discovery about the Ice Warrior was vitally important. Clent and the others must be told – and quickly!

*

In the laboratory, Jamie had at last given Victoria a turn in the vibro-chair. As the almost imperceptible tingling began she closed her eyes and smiled with childish delight. Jamie stood over her, his back to the great block of ice. Neither of them was aware that it had all but completely disintegrated, leaving the body once trapped inside it free and alive.

Suddenly, Victoria opened her eyes, looked past Jamie – and screamed. At the same moment, Jamie heard the power pack crash to the floor, and spun round to see what had caused the noise. The massive form of the Ice Warrior was not merely free of the ice block, but was looming over him, hideously threatening! His immediate reaction, keyed by Victoria's choked scream, was to protect her. Without hesitation, he threw himself against the motionless giant, in a vain attempt to grapple with that immense strength – but he might as well have been a wolfhound tackling a dinosaur. With one sweeping blow from its mighty arm, the Ice Warrior knocked him unconscious to the ground. With one great lumbering stride, the armoured giant reached the vibro-chair – but Victoria had already fainted. For a brief moment, the Ice Warrior gazed at her limp body, the breath seeming to hiss with difficulty through his strangely reptilian lips. He ponderously looked all around the room – as if searching for the best means of escape. Then, lifting Victoria as though she was no more than a feather, he strode past Jamie's fallen body, through the nearest doorway, and into the corridor beyond...

Clent and his subordinates were seated in a tight semi-circle around the table top formed by the ECCO control area. A stranger would have observed that the video-eyed communicator was not merely treated as a convenient information source, but was functioning as a member of the group. In fact, it had several jobs. Like an electronic secretary, it was taking minutes of the meeting; it produced relevant statistics when required, and it evaluated group decisions in the light of world policy. At the moment, however, it was passive. Clent was completing the summary of his confrontation with the Doctor.

'It took him just ninety seconds to propose and explain Ionisation,' he stated, 'and with no prior knowledge!'

Arden was impressed, but cautious. 'It took us and the World Academy of Scientists years.'

'And the computer three millisecs,' interrupted Miss Garrett. Brilliant though this stranger might be, he could never be superior to her beloved computer. Arden disagreed.

'It couldn't do anything without proper programming,' he pointed out shrewdly, much to Jan's annoyance. But Clent shared her absolute faith in the machine.

'I'd like an assessment from the computer,' he insisted, 'before we make any final decision about this... Doctor.'

'I agree,' nodded Miss Garrett. 'We have to be completely certain.'

'ECCO!' instructed Clent. The artificial head turned expectantly. 'State the work potential and group value of this new member of our team.'

The computer's answer was immediate and passionless.

More information needed for complete evaluation. Interim judgement: high IQ but undisciplined to unit's immediate needs. Possible use on research projects. Could be obstructive in certain subjective situations.'

The last sentence went largely unheard. At that moment, the door burst open and the Doctor stumbled rather breathlessly into the room. 'There you are!' he exclaimed.

'We've been waiting for you, Doctor,' Clent pointed out with icy formality. 'Perhaps you wouldn't mind sitting down?'

'I've been looking for you everywhere!' replied the Doctor. 'Why don't you label your doors, or something?'

'Perhaps you'd let us complete our official business before making unnecessary complaints about administration,' said Clent coldly.

'No, I'm afraid not,' insisted the Doctor. 'I've got something pretty important to tell you actually. It's about that thing in the block of ice.'

'The Ice Warrior!' exclaimed Arden anxiously. 'Has something happened to it?'

'We have more serious matters on hand than amateur archaeology!' interrupted Clent. But the Doctor was not to be shouted down.

'This is serious,' he continued grimly. 'It's the thing's helmet – it's not what we think it is.'

'You've discovered that it's a prehistoric drinking cup, I suppose,' said Clent sarcastically.

The Doctor was looking at Arden as he spoke. 'It has electronic connections,' he said.

There was a tense silence, as this remark struck home. Clent frowned. Was this stranger, dressed like a scavenger but with the brain of a scientist, a complete eccentric or, even worse, a practical joker? On the other hand, his face was deadly serious.

'What are you talking about, man?' he demanded, uncertainly.

Arden's amazement exploded into words. 'It's not possible! You must've made a mistake!'

'I'm quite sure.' The Doctor was almost apologetic. 'Of course, you do realise what this means?'

Clent said nothing, but it was obvious that thoughts were racing through his mind. Arden groped for an explanation.

'It must mean…' he paused, then plunged on, 'it *has* to mean its culture was even more advanced than we first thought!'

'So much more advanced,' remarked the Doctor drily, 'that they even had astronauts?'

'What!' exclaimed Clent.

'That headpiece of his,' observed the Doctor, 'it's not a warrior's tin hat, you know. It's a highly sophisticated space helmet!'

Miss Garrett firmly decided that the Doctor was having them on. What he was saying was impossible – and somebody had to tell him so!

'Don't you think you're jumping to conclusions, Doctor – for a scientist?' she said coolly. 'I mean to say – a prehistoric spaceman! It's ridiculous!'

Arden's face was shining with excitement. The implications were fantastic! 'If it's true,' he whispered, his mind in a turmoil… But the Doctor's next words brought him down to earth.

'If it's true,' the Doctor repeated grimly, 'the Ioniser programme here could be finished for good.'

Clent had the barest premonition of what the Doctor's warning could mean. But it was too startling to be admitted openly.

'In what way?' he asked, smiling. 'How can one deep-frozen body, no matter how many centuries old, affect our project? You're talking nonsense, my dear chap!'

The Doctor studied Clent's seemingly amused face, and understood why he didn't want to admit the truth. It really was an impossible dilemma – but it had to be faced. He sighed. He'd better explain, gently – as if to children.

'How did the Ice Warrior get there then?' The others remained silent, baffled. 'He didn't walk there, did he?'

Reluctantly, Clent answered. '*If* what you say is true... he must have arrived... by spaceship.'

'And where's that spaceship now, do you reckon?' enquired the Doctor gently. He answered his own question. 'In the glacier...'

Arden began to daydream again, his eyes shining with the possibilities. 'It could still be intact! The Ice Warrior showed no signs of damage or mutilation. They might not have crashed; they might have actually *landed* – to explore Earth!' He turned from Miss Garrett to Clent, almost begging them to share his exultation. 'Can't you see what it means? Intelligent contact with beings from another planet!'

The Doctor spoke more soberly. 'I think Leader Clent also sees the inherent dangers.'

Clent nodded grimly. 'The propulsion unit of the

spacecraft…' he began.

Jan, too, saw what the Doctor was getting at, and whispered, 'Could it be reactor powered?'

'Quite so, Miss Garrett,' applauded the Doctor. 'And if you were to use the Ioniser at anything like full power…'

'The heat…' she hesitated, then went on, 'the spaceship's reactor could go critical… and we'd have no way of preventing it from exploding…'

'The radiation…' Arden looked at the others, his face now full of anxiety. 'The whole area would be contaminated – possibly for centuries!'

'And what if we don't use the Ioniser – what happens then?' broke in Clent. 'We are part of a world plan! If we hold back, the whole operation must fail!'

'We could try holding it at minimal power,' suggested Jan.

'You know that won't work!' snapped Clent. 'It increases the risks of a power feed-back here, with a resulting explosion in our *own* reactor!'

At last it had been spelled out. While the others considered their desperate position, the Doctor murmured his apology.

'Sorry. But I thought you ought to know.'

'You were quite right to do so,' Clent acknowledged with a tired gesture. 'We must inform the computer, of course.'

Before he could take steps to do so, the doors clattered open, to reveal Jamie, still dazed. He clung desperately to the doorframe. A trickle of blood had dried on his forehead.

'Doctor!' he called out, his face tense with effort.

Within seconds, the Doctor had helped Jamie into the nearest chair. He saw at a glance that the cut on Jamie's head was no more than a graze. But it was obvious that something was seriously the matter. And where was Victoria? Jamie's breathless words explained everything – and added yet another amazing twist to the already desperate situation.

'It's that Warrior fellow!' he gasped. 'He's come alive!'

Both Clent and Miss Garrett were stunned into silence, but Arden cried out in disbelief. 'What!'

'I couldn't stop him. He packs a punch like a charging bull!'

'Victoria,' demanded the Doctor, 'where is she? Is she all right?'

Jamie looked at him, sober-faced, and shook his head miserably. 'I don't know,' he muttered. 'He took her with him!'

With Clent leading the way, it was only a matter of minutes before the group arrived at the laboratory. The scene spoke for itself: the trolley, empty but for a mass of crushed ice, the shattered power pack, and the overturned vibro-chair. The Ice Warrior's past had erupted into the present. Jamie, still dazed, sat down. While the others talked, the Doctor examined the trolley and the electrodes that had once been attached to the great ice block.

'There's something very strange about this,' he remarked.

Clent, utterly bewildered, was questioning Jamie. 'But what did you do to make it happen?'

'How do I know? We were just talking, and then I turned, and there he was – standing right over me!'

'It's impossible,' insisted Arden.

'For a human being, perhaps...' said the Doctor, mysteriously.

Clent stared at him, uncomprehending.

'Look at this table,' the Doctor pointed to its surface. It was cracked and bubbled – as though scorched by fire.

'But that would take immense heat!' exclaimed Clent.

'The electricity—' offered Jamie.

Arden rejected this. 'I used a low voltage, deliberately!'

'But a high current, I believe,' pointed out the Doctor.

'Yes... but it was safe – there was no fire risk!' retorted the geologist.

'It isn't necessarily a question of actual fire,' explained the Doctor. 'Suppose that current flowed through a high resistance. What would be the result?'

'Extremely high temperatures,' replied Jan. 'You mean, that thing...'

'I said it wasn't human, didn't I?' the Doctor reminded her. 'In my opinion, the sudden build-up of heat shocked him back into neural activity.'

'And what about Victoria?' demanded Jamie, clearheaded and alert once more. 'What can we do to save *her*?'

A surge of guilt flowed over the Doctor's mind. He faced Jamie tensely, the scientific problem forgotten.

'You're right, Jamie. We've got to find her! They couldn't have got far!'

Clent, too, had reacted sharply to the reminder that an undesirable alien menace was loose within the Base

53

complex; less important was its helpless hostage. He moved quickly to the video-communicator.

'Danger. Red alert!' he snapped to all channels within the Base. 'Intruders within Base perimeter. Capture and control – priority one!'

But Jamie wasn't impressed. 'What good's that? Suppose they're already out of it? We've got to go after them – now!'

'My dear chap, I'm very sorry, but we're down to emergency personnel only. I cannot release men to go wandering off outside this Base. It'd be madness!'

'But the girl's life may be at stake!' added the Doctor. 'You *have* to make a search party available!'

Jan Garrett saw Clent's mouth tighten stubbornly. No matter how much the Doctor argued, the Leader had made up his mind. But there was one possible way out.

'Leader Clent,' she suggested calmly, 'we must inform the computer.' She paused, knowing he had to agree, then went on, 'It could soon tell us whether it is possible to reallocate the work schedule to release a rescue party.'

The others watched tensely as Clent considered Jan's shrewd suggestion. He reluctantly nodded his head.

'Very well, we will put it to the computer...'

Unknown to Clent and the Doctor, Victoria was being held prisoner only a hundred yards away. At the first sound of the security alarm, the Ice Warrior had entered the nearest convenient bolt hole – a medical store room.

Victoria had still been unconscious when they had taken cover. Coming round now, she had no idea where she

54

was. All that she could see from the corner where she lay huddled, was the gigantic form of the Ice Warrior. He was standing by the door, listening intently. The distant alarm call stopped abruptly. Seemingly satisfied, the creature now turned towards Victoria – and she saw his cruel face clearly for the first time.

Her throat became so tight with fear that she could scarcely gasp… The so-called armour of the helmet-head and massive body was in fact tough, and reptilian in substance – but unlike animal eyes, its hard glass-covered eye sockets revealed no emotion. Only a vaguely flickering light illuminated their dark depths.

Like the eyes, the creature's ears looked mechanical in design – electronic, as the Doctor had said. But the mouth was different: mobile, leathery, lizard-like. It seemed to be forever struggling to snatch in precious air, with the result that every breath, every word it uttered, hissed snake-like from that menacing head. From the huge shoulders downwards, the armoured skin took on the shape of a great protective shell.

Victoria noticed with a shudder that instead of hands, or even webbed, reptilian claws, the arms ended in what looked like metallic clamps. And from the right forearm, compact and sleek, but as though part of the creature's physical anatomy, projected a strange, tubular device – rather like the telescopic sights of a rifle. Victoria had no time for further speculation. The Ice Warrior was now looming over her, cruel and menacing.

'Stand!' it commanded.

Victoria forced herself upright. Her knees were like

water. Only by spreading herself back against the wall could she safely stay on her feet. She tried to keep the terror out of her voice; her chin tilted upwards bravely.

'Who are you?' she demanded, looking up defiantly at the warrior head. At first, she heard only the eerie sound of its hissing breath; Victoria shivered beneath its dark, inscrutable gaze. What sort of creature was part reptile, part machine?

'Where are you from?' she cried out boldly, knowing all the while that if the creature made another sudden move, she would probably faint. The response from the creature made Victoria's eyes grow round with wonder.

'My name… is Varga…' came the slow, faltering reply. 'My home… is the Red Planet!'

It can't be true, Victoria thought to herself desperately. But she forced her voice to frame the question, 'Mars?'

Varga nodded proudly. Unearthly as he was, everything about him echoed the famous legends that Victoria had heard about the god of war; his pride, his strength and his savagery in battle. But this was a living, hideous alien – not a Greek god. And one who had been dead and buried in the glacier's ice only hours ago. For a moment, curiosity overcame her fear.

'But you were dead!' exclaimed Victoria. 'How did you come back to life?' She stopped and flinched as Varga gestured angrily.

'Enough questions!' he hissed furiously. 'Give me answers!'

'Why should I?' She never had liked being ordered about – even when frightened. But her defiance wavered.

The Ice Warrior was now pointing the strange tubular device straight at her head.

'Answers!' came the insistent demand. Victoria nodded dumbly. The Ice Warrior continued. 'How long was I trapped in the ice?'

'I don't know—'Victoria started to say, then remembered that answers were compulsory. 'One of the scientists here thinks you must have been inside the glacier since the First Ice Age...' she faltered, hardly able to believe it herself, '... thousands of years ago.'

The Ice Warrior hissed with astonishment. 'As long ago as that?' He paused in wonderment, and then quickly demanded, 'They found nothing else?'

Alarm flared suddenly in Victoria's mind. She steeled herself to look into his expressionless face. 'You mean... there are others like you?' she whispered.

The Ice Warrior lowered his arm, and stood strangely rigid. Victoria sensed the brooding change within Varga's mind as he cast back through centuries of time, struggling to remember.

'We were hovering... over the frozen lands. A sudden turbulence... our spacecraft crashed at the foot of the Ice Mountain.' He paused. His memory was clearing. 'We went outside our craft to investigate. The ice mountain shook... split open... swallowed us in a great whirlwind of snow, and there was only darkness.'

He fell silent. Only the gentle labouring of his breath told Victoria anything of his state of mind. She spoke with sympathy.

'The others with you,' murmured Victoria, 'did they all

die – trapped inside the glacier?'

Varga drew himself up proudly, and giving the staccato, dry cough that passed in his race for laughter, replied harshly. 'If they are dead as I was... then they can be freed – and made to live!'

The full meaning of what Varga was saying didn't strike home to Victoria immediately. She could only see the impossibility of ever finding Varga's companions – let alone recovering them from the glacier. 'You'll never be able to get them out by yourself!' she declared.

'You do not yet understand my capabilities,' he murmured harshly. 'But I will need your help!'

'*My* help?' questioned Victoria, surprised. 'How?'

'Tell me... how I was brought to life? What is the process? What did these Earthling scientists do?'

'How do I know?' said Victoria in exasperation. 'I'm not one of them.'

'You saw, you were with them. Tell me!'

'Why ask me? Why not let me take you to the scientists – to the Doctor? They'll help you!'

'I am a stranger – an alien. Why should they help me? They would take me prisoner – keep me as a scientific curiosity – and leave my men for dead in the ice.'

'They wouldn't!' exclaimed Victoria. But this was no human castaway she was speaking to – this was a Martian warlord.

'With my men, I can talk from strength – not beg.' He coughed abruptly – a sharp, sneering rasp – and Victoria shivered at the menace in the sound, as he continued. 'Then we shall decide!'

'Decide…?' Victoria's alarm was gradually changing to panic. 'Decide what?'

There was no mistaking the grim confidence in Varga's voice. 'Whether to return to our own planet,' he replied sternly, 'or conquer yours!'

In the great hall, Clent had finished putting the situation to ECCO. The others were gathered about him, tensely waiting for its judgement.

'Those are the relevant factors,' finished Clent. 'How should we proceed?'

Jamie could keep quiet no longer, and blurted out in anger, 'How's a machine to know?'

'Be quiet, Jamie,' admonished the Doctor, as the crisp voice of the computer began to discharge its answer.

'*The ionisation programme should continue as instructed – but the presence of an alien spacecraft must be investigated.*'

The computer paused fractionally. Clent's look of bland superiority changed to a frown.

'But how can we?' he asked the computer. 'Our reduced manpower—'

The computer chose to ignore Clent, and continued coldly. '*Suspected fissionable material must take priority,*' it clipped out. '*Glacial status can be held for limited period.*'

'But what about Victoria?' interrupted Jamie.

'*The emergency operating schedule has been rearranged to free one scientist for the investigation,*' continued the machine calmly. '*In the present circumstances, the nominated member should be scientist Arden. Effect these instructions immediately.*'

The computer fell silent. Clent turned to Arden, who could barely hide his excitement.

'You heard what's to be done, Arden. Do you think you can handle it?'

'He'll never cope with that Ice Warrior by himself!' insisted Jamie.

'I could do with a security guard,' agreed Arden nervously.

'The computer has nominated one man only,' snapped Clent irritably. 'It will have to be enough!'

'What about me?' asked Jamie eagerly. 'Let me go with him!'

Clent frowned, about to give a sharp retort, but the Doctor cut in quickly. 'He's a capable lad – and he's not on your staff. He's extra.'

Clent studied the Doctor thoughtfully, then shrugged. It was true: this boy was surplus, and as such, not Clent's responsibility. He was also something of a troublemaker – better out of the way.

'Very well. As the Doctor is going to help us with the Ioniser, the boy can go.' As Jamie glanced triumphantly at the Doctor, Clent scowled. 'But there must be no delay!' he insisted harshly. 'Go – now!'

Jan Garrett smoothly explained Clent's apprehension. 'The sooner we know whether there *is* a nuclear reactor buried inside the glacier, the better.'

'Aye, mebbe,' replied Jamie curtly. 'But our Victoria's important too, ye know.'

Clent turned on him savagely.

'Don't you realise, boy? The fate of the whole of Europe

could be at stake! That's what's important – not this prehistoric freak of Arden's, nor the girl! She'll just have to take her chance!'

4

Back from the Dead

Storr gritted his teeth against the pain. Penley threw a quick glance at his drawn, pallid face, then deftly completed the task of bandaging the now swollen arm. It was a bad break; the bone-torn muscle was rapidly going septic, and Storr wasn't far from a coma. But it was his own pigheaded stubbornness that had brought about his present critical state. Penley knotted the make-shift bandage tight, and felt Storr wince.

'What're you trying to do? Cripple me?'

'Sorry, old chap,' soothed Penley. He tried to make his surly patient more comfortable. 'The trouble with you, you know, is that you will insist on being stupid.'

Storr turned his face away. He hated admitting he was wrong – but he had to be honest. 'How was I to know it'd get infected?' he growled, then sank back weakly.

Penley looked round at Storr's bizarre den – the abandoned Victorian conservatory in which, years before, Storr had established his plant museum. How much longer would it last, he wondered? How long would it take before the ice – which was again rumbling ominously outside – was in there with them?

'You should've listened to me in the first place,' said

Penley, 'shouldn't you?'

'And given you the chance to stuff me with anti-this, and anti-that?' grumbled Storr. 'I'd've been flat on my back for months…!'

'Whereas now,' observed Penley drily, 'you're fighting fit, of course.'

Storr rose to the bait as usual. 'Someone's got to do things!'

'Well that someone isn't going to be you for a while yet. And it serves you right.'

'It's nothing!' snapped Storr. 'I'll pull through!'

He gazed at his precious plants through a haze of pain, desperately trying to concentrate his mind.

'… how it was before they killed off all the plants,' he gabbled, half-smiling. 'There would have been *Spring*, then – fruit, on trees, waiting to be picked…' His ravaged face tightened into bitterness once more. 'Now… you damned scientists – destructive meddlers!' His anger subsided again. 'Killed all the plants… and flowers…'

Penley could see that he was slipping into a coma. Soon, there would be no wood left from their precious stock, and without that warmth, the deadly cold would start to creep into Storr's haven. He had to act – and quickly. He stood up, and started to put on the heavy skins for snow travel. His quick and decisive movements woke Storr. 'What're you doing, you fool!' mumbled the half-conscious man.

'The Base,' replied Penley curtly.

Storr tried to rise, but he had no strength. He fell back helplessly, but his eyes burned with fever and accusation. 'You're going to turn me in… like a dirty coward. I don't want… rehabilitation… Africa…' He was nearly out, but still he protested. 'Never trust… scientists.'

Penley turned. 'It's for your idiotic sake that I'm going! For drugs! And if I don't get them…' He looked down at the unconscious body, 'you're as good as dead!'

'Think!' commanded the Ice Warrior in that strange, fierce whisper. 'Tell me what it was they used to give my body life!'

Victoria could see that there was no escape. But what could she tell him when she knew so little herself?

'I don't know what it was called, so how *can* I tell you?' she explained desperately.

But Varga wasn't going to be satisfied that easily. 'Describe it!' he hissed sharply.

Victoria tried hard to remember what the scientist Arden had done to the great ice block – but it was difficult. She hadn't really been paying attention at the time. The body inside the ice had been the subject of everyone's fascination – and now here it was, alive and menacing, holding her prisoner!

'It was a sort of… small black box,' she suggested vaguely.

'Go on!' demanded Varga with an urgent gesture. 'Explain how it worked!'

'It had wires,' recalled Victoria hesitantly, then blurted out 'and they connected the wires to the ice. It made a funny, quiet sort of noise – and nobody knew you were going to come to life, but you just did!' She paused, breathless and afraid.

But it was enough for the Ice Warrior to understand. His great clamp-like fist pointed towards his armoured chest. 'A power source,' he hissed wonderingly. 'High resistance… great heat… and then – life!' He swung round to face Victoria, and pointed the device at her terrified face.

'This room we came from,' he whispered harshly, 'I wish to return to it – now!'

Victoria's face brightened. 'I'll tell you how to get there!' The Ice Warrior wasn't taken in by her sudden co-operation.

'You will take me there,' he commanded, gripping her arm. 'You will help me find the power unit. With that my men, too, can be brought back from the dead…'

Desperately, Victoria searched her mind for excuses, all the while aware of the numbing pressure on her wrist, and the delicate menace of the device on Varga's arm.

'But we'll have to go along the corridor,' she pointed out quickly. 'And supposing someone sees you holding me prisoner?'

'Then I shall be forced to kill them,' hissed the Martian warlord calmly. 'And you also, if you attempt to call for help.' He held the device between Victoria's frightened eyes. She swallowed hard, but spoke bravely.

'What is it?' she asked fearfully.

'It is a sonic destructor. To put it simply, it will disintegrate your brain with sound waves.'

She looked at the Martian, eyes wide.

'All right,' she said, trying to hide the fear in her voice. 'Are you ready now?'

Varga silently gestured for her to lead the way. Victoria

slowly opened the door, praying desperately that they would meet nobody on their way to the medicare centre. She paused for a moment, surveying the corridor outside. It was deserted. Varga shuffled close behind her, urging her onward. Blindly, she obeyed. The alternative was too horrible to think about…

Penley had approached the same corridor from the terrace. Huddled in a shadowy corner, he was contemplating his next move. The corridor was unusually quiet – without even the normal security guard. What could it all mean? Was something really wrong – or was it some sort of trap? He listened intently. In the far distance, he could hear the high pitch of machinery which had once been so familiar to him. The Ioniser was still functioning then – though not for much longer, he thought grimly. But all that was Clent's problem now. The immediate goal was to get into the medicare centre and select the drugs needed to save Storr's life.

Suddenly, he froze. His ears had caught a sound – subtly different, puzzling – coming along the corridor towards him: slow, ponderous, shuffling – and accompanied by a lighter, more timid step. He looked cautiously out from the shadows that concealed him – and his eyebrows shot up in amazement.

Advancing cautiously towards the doorway of the medicare centre was a girl – but it was her companion that had shocked Penley. He had seen nothing like it on Earth! Immense – eight feet tall at least – it looked almost prehistoric. A glint of light suddenly caught its helmet and clumsy mechanical hands. Penley barely managed to stifle a gasp. His mind raced, throwing up a flood of questions. What was it? What was such a creature doing inside the Base? Who on earth was the girl?

Then, Penley saw the tight look of terror on the girl's young face – barely more than a child, he realised, as she moved closer. Her slender wrist was gripped by the monster who was hulking beside her. They stopped outside the medicare doorway.

Then, as the reptilian giant biped thrust the doors open with one blow of his massive arm, the girl looked about her desperately, before being dragged inside. Her eyes widened as she saw Penley. His first reaction was to rush forward to help – but something in her face stopped the movement almost before it began. Although her eyes pleaded with him, her head gave the slightest of negative movements – stay away! Penley was soon to know why. As though angered by the girl's reluctance to go through the medicare doors, the monster pointed his free arm directly at her head. The gesture was unmistakable, and Penley caught a clear glimpse of the strange tubular device… The girl obediently stumbled into the room and out of sight, followed by the massive creature. Once more the corridor was silent and empty, leaving Penley totally unnerved and desperate to know what to do next.

Inside the medicare centre Varga paused, taking in the room and its complex equipment. On the far side of the room stood the trolley that had once borne his lifeless body. It was slopping with water and fragments of melting ice. Satisfied, he released Victoria from his iron grasp.

'This is the place…' he hissed, then gestured curtly at

Victoria, who was standing frightened and helpless in the centre of the room. 'The black box!' he exclaimed. 'Find it! Quickly!'

A rare calm reigned in the control room complex. For the first time in weeks, the Ioniser hadn't kept everyone in a state of permanent tension. Jan moved along the ranks of monitor technicians, and felt almost elated. This was how their great project should be – totally under control.

She glanced across at the ECCO conference table, where Clent and the Doctor were studying circuit blueprints on the videoscreen. Could one man make such a difference, she wondered, as she studied the clownish figure seated by Leader Clent. Her respect for his intelligence far outweighed her displeasure at his irreverent treatment of her or his impudent smile. She also knew that Clent had accepted the Doctor as his equal – in brainpower if not in authority. And this had been the most important factor of all in stabilising the near-to-panic atmosphere. She sighed inwardly. If only Penley could see the place like this instead of as it had been the day he stormed out under a hail of sarcasm from Clent...

Clent looked at the Doctor, who was concentrating on the videoscreen by his side. 'I still say it needs an expert,' commented the Doctor, nodding towards the elaborate circuitry designs on the videoscreen. 'Can't you afford one?'

Clent's face stiffened. Had the Doctor been reading his mind? 'I choose not to,' he clipped.

'Why?'

'You are not here to question my decisions! You have no authority.'

'I know,' agreed the Doctor, unruffled. 'I'm here to help – if I so choose.' He smiled. 'I think we should trust each other, don't you?'

With an effort, Clent controlled the instinctive resentment he felt whenever this bitter subject cropped up: a rational explanation should clear this matter up once and for all, he decided. He didn't realise that behind the Doctor's seemingly innocent and trusting gaze was a probing intelligence that could – if need be – winkle the truth out of a giant clam.

'You'll appreciate,' stated Clent, 'the importance of this mission. I was chosen because I never fail. My record is one hundred per cent success. And I've handled some big projects, I assure you, Doctor.' He paused, and frowned. 'As always, I hand-picked my team… but for once, I made a vital mistake…'

'This chap Penley?' suggested the Doctor, knowingly.

Clent nodded. 'The best man in Europe for Ionisation studies… but as it turned out, hopelessly temperamental!'

The Doctor looked at Clent shrewdly. The Leader's defensive reaction had already revealed what was wrong. 'Temperamental,' the Doctor queried gently, 'or individual? Creative scientists have to be allowed some freedom of thought, you know, otherwise—'

Clent cut in angrily, stung by the way in which the Doctor had hit the nail on the head. 'Creative poppycock! When Penley walked out of here, he publicly proclaimed himself to be criminally irresponsible!'

'You don't think, then, that what he did could have been a simple gesture of protest?'

'He was always protesting! This unit is a team – a team with a mission! If we fail, how can others expect to succeed?'

'And it'll be your name that suffers, of course,' replied the Doctor keenly. 'And that's important to you, isn't it?'

Suddenly Clent was on the defensive. 'I lead the team, but I depend on the experts that I select. With the exception of Penley, my judgement was sound. But others won't see it that way. They'll only mark up the failure!'

'So you really need this chap Penley.'

'No! I do *not* need Penley!' Then he added hastily, 'But I do need an equivalent brain to take over from where that… traitor left off! Normally, it would take months to train up a stranger.' His face had a look of desperation. 'There simply isn't time – that's the truth of the matter! And that's why we need *you*!'

'I'll do what I can. But I think you ought to understand that personally I prefer trusting human beings rather than computers.'

Clent's face grew stern and proud. His hand came to rest on ECCO's control panel. 'I trust nobody, Doctor. Human emotions are too unreliable.' Suddenly, as though at the flick of a switch, he dismissed the whole subject from his mind, and became brisk and purposeful once more. 'If you require any further data, Miss Garrett will obtain it for you. I'll go and check that there is a working area cleared ready for you in the medicare centre. Perhaps you'd like to join me there when you're ready?' With that he strode off.

The Doctor stared after him, and thoughtfully shook his head...

Varga was becoming more and more furious. Victoria, sensing that his anger was increasing, searched ever more hurriedly for the vital power pack. At the sound of smashing glass, she spun round. With one sweep of his mighty arm, Varga had cleared a nearby bench of its chemical apparatus. He turned to her, his breath coming in fearful gasps.

'Where is this power source!' he snarled, moving towards her with mighty strides. 'Do not try to trick me! If it is not here—'

His threat was lost as he overturned a cupboard in his effort to reach Victoria. As it fell, a jumble of equipment fell out – among it several power packs. Varga stopped, and studied the confusion of gear at his feet. He looked up at Victoria, whose tense face showed her relief. She nodded.

'Yes,' she whispered. 'Those are the ones.'

She watched as the Ice Warrior picked up a couple by their leads, and began to examine them triumphantly. What would he do now? As though in answer to her unspoken thought, Varga turned his mighty head towards her and spoke.

'You will come with me to the Ice Mountain,' he hissed, and grabbed her unresisting arm. But Victoria's eyes were staring past the Ice Warrior to the doorway. Standing there, his face stunned with disbelief, was Clent. Victoria screamed a warning – but too late. In an instant, Varga had turned, seen Clent, and swung into action.

Fortunately for the scientist, Varga's weapon arm was

holding the precious power packs. Instead of using the sonic destructor, the Ice Warrior swung the power packs by their leads, like a medieval ball and chain. Clent, having no chance to dodge the swift, savage blow, slumped to the floor without even a cry. Victoria stared in horror at his crumpled body.

'You've… killed him,' she whispered.

'Come!' Varga replied harshly – but Victoria had fainted. Pausing only to sweep up her limp body in the crook of his mighty arm, the Martian strode over the fallen scientist and through the doors leading to the corridor and freedom.

Penley had seen Clent arrive and enter the medicare centre. Minutes later, the reptilian giant burst out into the corridor, carrying the girl on one arm and a tangled bundle of power packs in the other cruel fist. Once he was out of sight, Penley dashed into the medicare room, to find Clent sprawled and bleeding from a head wound. Crouching by him, Penley felt expertly for a pulse. He nodded with satisfaction and then, moving casually across to a compact automat machine that dispensed pharmaceutical components, dialled the correct formula. Almost immediately, several phials and syringes appeared in the tray beneath. Taking them up, Penley now dialled a fresh formula, a light smile playing on his lips. The mixture duly arrived, and he turned to deal with Clent – only to find the Doctor kneeling by the unconscious body, head to its chest, listening for the tell-tale heartbeat. The Doctor straightened up, but stayed kneeling; Penley moved to his side. For a brief moment, the two bizarrely dressed men solemnly looked at each other without fear or anger. Penley smiled faintly, and handed the phial to the Doctor for his approval.

'He isn't dead,' he remarked casually. 'I was going to give him a whiff of this.'

The Doctor sniffed at the open phial warily – then pulled a sickened face. 'Revolting!' Almost gleefully, he thrust it beneath Clent's unresisting nose. 'This should do the trick very nicely,' he chuckled, then looked from the cut on Clent's forehead to Penley. 'Did you do this?'

Penley shook his head. 'I've come close to it at times. In fact, I've never seen him looking so peaceful.'

'He'll be all right. Did you see anything of what happened?'

'A great monstrous-looking creature – reptilian biped. But not prehistoric – possibly a robot.'

The Doctor studied Penley keenly; his summary displayed scientific deduction of the highest quality. But there was a more urgent question in the Doctor's mind. 'Was there a girl with this creature – captive, or under duress?'

Penley nodded. 'Yes,' he frowned. 'She was unconscious.' He saw the glare of accusation in the Doctor's eyes, and hurriedly explained. 'I couldn't have stopped that giant. No one man could.' He glanced down at Clent. 'Anyway, I came here to get drugs – to save a man's life. I don't intend getting caught.'

His eyes held the Doctor's gaze challengingly. Mild though the ragged intruder appeared, the Doctor knew that he would let little stand in the way of his original purpose. It explained something of Clent's bitter attitude, too.

'Look, Penley,' the Doctor said hesitatingly.

74

Penley looked suddenly wary. 'You know about me, do you? My dreadful escapades in computer-land…'

'Whatever happened in the past,' declared the Doctor earnestly, 'they need you here now. They're in desperate trouble!'

'Needing isn't getting. I'm free of their problems for good. And I've a friend who'll die unless I get back quickly.'

'The problems here are yours as well! It's your world that's threatened, isn't it?'

Penley smiled gently, and tapped the side of his head with one finger. 'My world's up here, my friend – strictly private and no admittance. Clent can keep all this!' He looked keenly at the Doctor, almost daring him to interfere, then spoke quietly. 'I'm leaving. All right?'

'I'm sure you've got good reasons, old chap,' the Doctor replied soberly. 'Good luck.'

Penley reached the door, then turned and smiled. 'Nice to meet someone who hasn't been got at,' he said cheerfully, and was gone.

A quiet groan came from the floor by the Doctor's feet. He looked down at Clent's body with an air of pained surprise. 'Good heavens, Clent, I'd forgotten all about you!' He crouched, and thrust the evil-smelling phial under the Leader's nose once more. Coughing and spluttering, Clent struggled to sit upright, and avoid the pungent fumes. The movement brought an awareness of throbbing pain in his head. He looked at the Doctor with a dazed expression, before the full memory of what had happened flooded back.

'The Ice Warrior!' he exclaimed – then, wincing, spoke more quietly, though still with urgency. 'Where is he?'

'Gone. And he's taken Victoria with him.'

'But why?' asked Clent. 'Why here? They'd already escaped once!' His hand went tentatively to his skull, and gently fingered the scalp wound. 'He hit me with a power pack.'

The Doctor looked thoughtful. Almost absent-mindedly, he helped Clent to his feet. But his brain was working furiously.

'A power pack…' he mused aloud. 'Like the one that Arden used to unfreeze him?'

Clent nodded – then wished he hadn't, as the dizzying pain made his head swim again. He steadied himself, then pointed towards the wreckage of the overturned cupboard.

'Those. But why?' He groaned. 'What's that creature up to – and what made it come back here to Base?'

'My dear chap,' observed the Doctor drily, 'I think you'll find it never actually left in the first place.' He looked thoughtfully about the room. 'He must've stayed hidden while we set up the security search, then waited for his opportunity when the alarm was cancelled.' He looked hard at Clent. 'This Ice Warrior isn't a fool, Clent. He's clever. And he didn't intend to leave here empty-handed either!'

'You mean he took the girl as a hostage?'

Before the Doctor could tell Clent of the fear that was in his mind, the doors burst open and Miss Garrett entered. Her face looked tense. Close behind her came Arden and Jamie, both now dressed for their journey to the ice face.

They stopped short at the sight of Clent and the wrecked laboratory.

'Leader Clent, what has happened?' demanded Jan, hurrying towards him. 'Are you all right?'

'I was attacked by that confounded ice-age monster of yours, Arden!' The pain in his head forced him to control his anger, but his voice was harsh. 'I want it found – immediately! And captured!'

Jan looked in dismay towards Arden, then faced Clent bravely. 'We've just had a report from the outer perimeter,' she said. 'The… creature has smashed its way out – and it's got the girl.'

'If we go now we can soon catch up with it!' exclaimed Jamie. 'But they won't let us without your say-so.'

'If you'd got ready when I told you—' rasped Clent, but Arden quickly cut in to defend the Scots lad.

'We've prepared ourselves as quickly as we could, Clent! If we'd been any quicker, we'd have got outside *before* the creature.'

'It's heading for the glacier, I'd say,' said the Doctor, 'and it's taken at least one power pack with it – and, of course, Victoria.'

'A power pack?' asked Jamie. 'What for?'

It was Arden who offered the solution that had already crossed the Doctor's mind. 'He's going to try and bring the others back to life!' His eyes blazed with excitement. 'There are others like him up there – there must be!'

'Arden,' interrupted Clent coldly, 'you were given the task of establishing the presence of an alien energy unit – not a menagerie! And I would prefer positive facts,' he added cuttingly, 'not schoolboy speculation!'

'Then what are we waiting for?' demanded Jamie restlessly. 'Let's go!'

'Not until dawn breaks, lad,' said Arden. 'It won't be long,' he added, seeing the dismay on the boy's face.

'Stalking the Ice Warrior by night'd be impossible, Jamie,' the Doctor pointed out. 'He's no fool—'

'But he's got Victoria!' protested Jamie fiercely.

'As a hostage, lad,' insisted the Doctor patiently. 'He wouldn't hump her all the way to the glacier if she wasn't going to be useful in some way, would he?'

'Then you reckon she'll be safe?' Even when the reassurance came from the Doctor, Jamie wasn't entirely convinced. But in the circumstances, it looked as though he had no choice.

'Of course,' replied the Doctor, forcing himself to sound cheerful. 'Now that all your gear is ready, you can set out at first light. And it isn't as if we don't know where he's going, is it?'

Clent, now fully recovered, cut in sharply. 'How many times do I have to remind you, Doctor,' he snapped, 'that we are not chasing monsters all over that ice mountain!'

'You really are very dense sometimes, Clent old chap,' observed the Doctor. 'With any luck, this creature will do our job for us! If there *is* a spacecraft, he'll lead us to it. Don't you see?' Seeing the grudging agreement on Clent's face, he added, 'And as for digging his chums out of the glacier, it'll take him ages bare-handed and alone! Isn't that so, Arden?'

Arden nodded, remembering how long it had taken

Davis, using the best of equipment. But his eyes met the Doctor's. He was suddenly aware that he wasn't alone in wondering what other surprises the Ice Warrior might have in store for his human opponents...

Victoria didn't regain consciousness until she found herself sprawling and spluttering in the skin-tingling freshness of a moonlit snowdrift. She scrambled to her feet almost automatically, dusted the snow from her clothes, turned to look at her surroundings – and choked on a scream.

The Ice Warrior was standing massively silhouetted against the night sky. His dark-screened eyes, eerie and menacing, glowed faintly as he turned slowly in a tight arc, scanning the surface of the glacier before him. A tiny circle of light pulsed regularly on his broad chest, and simultaneously a soft electronic ping – like an echo-sounder's – could be heard. One moment the giant creature stood motionless, the next he strode forward to the ice face, and gouged out a great chunk of ice with his huge clamp-shaped hand.

Victoria realised that this was her chance. While Varga studied the surface of the glacier, she prepared to make a silent escape – but she hadn't reckoned with the fragments of loose ice half-buried in the snow. At the first step, her ankle twisted, her foothold gave way, and with a sharp cry, she found herself sprawled helplessly at the feet of the Ice Warrior. She waited for him to show his anger – but he seemed almost preoccupied. Slowly, Victoria got to her feet, and backed away into the shelter of a vertical crevasse, with Varga's harsh whisper in her ears.

'Do not try to escape,' he hissed. 'You are not equipped for survival!'

He was right, of course. Sheltered from the keening wind, Victoria shivered and realised how small her chances would be out there on the open snow plain which stretched away into a silver whiteness under the cold eye of the moon. Here at least there was a possibility of staying alive – if only as Varga's prisoner. She stared back at those strangely glowing eyes, and spoke bravely.

'Where are we? At the glacier?'

'Yes,' Varga whispered, and sounded pleased. 'I have located the position of my men inside the ice. At last!'

Victoria was puzzled. Obviously the Ice Warrior had used some sort of detection device. But how had he known where to start in the first place? As though in reply to her question, Varga pointed to the crevasse in which Victoria crouched.

'The place where you stand,' he whispered, with no sign of misted breath showing on the frosted air, 'is where your scientists cut me free.' Wonderingly, Victoria looked all about her. She saw the regular grooves of a boring tool or drill, and frowned. If it had taken that sort of equipment to carve Varga from the living ice, how could he possibly hope to release his buried companions? She shivered again and started to stamp her feet and beat her hands together. If she stood still for much longer, she'd end up frozen inside the glacier herself!

'Do not waste energy,' commanded the Ice Warrior softly, and indicated that Victoria should move away from the ice face and stand by his side. At first, she objected.

'I'll freeze to death unless I keep my circulation going. At least I'm out of the wind in this cranny!'

'You will maintain your Earthling body temperature by helping me,' ordered the Martian.

'What are you going to do?' asked Victoria in surprise. How on earth did he expect her to help?

'I must release my comrades,' Varga replied. 'Then, when your friends come after us, we shall have a surprise ready...'

Irritated, Victoria didn't notice the quiet threat in Varga's words. She still couldn't understand what the Ice Warrior was going to do. 'But you'll never break that ice apart with your bare hands!' she cried petulantly. 'Arden used a heavy drill to get *you* out. Any other way is impossible!'

Without replying, Varga drew her to his side and into a position facing the glacier. Making a surprisingly delicate adjustment to the device on his right forearm with his massive fist, he pointed the device at the ice. The tip of the device pulsed with light – then, as Victoria watched in amazement, the rock-hard ice face began to disintegrate and shatter. Without tools, without even touching the surface of the ice, Varga was freeing his comrades as easily as carving a block of salt with a penknife...

Breathless from ploughing his way through the deep, soft snowdrifts leading up to the glacier face, Penley paused to take refuge from the vicious sting of the wind. Storr would have battled onwards uncomplainingly, of course – but Penley was honest enough to admit his weaknesses.

Besides, it was unwise to travel at night through the near silent landscape of these hills without halting and listening every now and then. The snow buried not only the ground and ice beneath it, but also every sound: wolves and bears moved quietly enough at the best of times, but under cover of the snow blanket they gained an edge of surprise that could be deadly. It paid to keep your ears open and your eyes sharp. It also paid to conserve your energy, thought Penley – especially when one of the team was flat on his back and totally incapable. Still, he thought, Storr's past the danger stage now; whatever the big man might rave about scientists and their hocus-pocus drugs, it was that very magic that had saved him. Penley had left him sleeping deeply – but with all trace of the burning fever gone. Twenty-four hours more, and the old pirate would be himself again; in time the bone would heal, strongly if not perfect. It was while Storr was out of service, undergoing repair, Penley smiled to himself, that he could tackle what was in his own mind.

There was a mystery afoot, involving the strange, warrior-like alien, the girl – and the scruffy-looking stranger he'd met in the medicare laboratory. Very odd, that one – what was he doing at the Base? How was it that he knew so much about Clent, and the problems that idiot brought on himself? Why had he asked him to come back to the Base? The man had a sense of humour, too... and that was unusual in itself. What was his link with the girl – and the creature from the ice?

He was certain that the ungainly monster he'd seen had something to do with Arden's excavations at the glacier face;

and there had only been one way to satisfy his questioning mind: go and investigate.

Penley lurched forward through the drifting snow, moving diagonally across the slope that would bring him close to the excavation site. But at the top of the wind-skimmed ridge, he paused and crouched, his eyes squinting into the wind, hardly able to believe what he saw.

The usually smooth curve of the glacier, instead of gleaming dully in the fading moonlight, glinted and sparkled like a frozen waterfall. In front of the shattered crystalline wall, ankle deep in ice fragments, towered the alien creature. Its arm was pointed at the ice face and, even at this distance the whine of some unseen device could be heard, faint but jarring to the ear. And as Penley watched, great frozen gouts of ice spurted and crumpled away, as though struck by a gigantic, invisible hammer! The creature was carving its way into the heart of the glacier!

Penley shaded his eyes and peered harder into the stinging spume of snow. Now he could make out the girl – apparently helping, though without much enthusiasm. But it was what stood beyond, gaunt and gleaming in the thin light of the dying moon, that caught Penley's eye and held it in unbelieving amazement. Like prehistoric stone monoliths, carved and dragged from the face of the glacier, towered four immense blocks of ice.

At last the searing whine of the sonic weapon ceased. With a series of great heaves, Varga tore the last remaining block of ice free of the glacier, and dragged it across to the others. The five gleaming crags loomed menacingly against the night sky; Victoria seemed to flinch from their cold power. Varga strode proudly up to them, and struck the fractured ice with his great fist.

'It is done,' he hissed, elated. 'They are free!'

He wheeled to face Victoria, and snapped out his orders. 'Bring the power packs to me!'

She could do nothing but obey. Snatching them from her, he deftly placed the electrodes at key points on the first two blocks of ice. They began to hum ominously. Varga faced his comrades boldly, and barked a command at their lifeless forms.

'Awake from the dead!'

5

The Omega Factor

Dawn at last. Outside the Base airlock, the equipment that Arden and Jamie would need for their investigation was already packed aboard the sleek form of the airsled. It included all the usual snowtrek survival gear: drilling tools, power packs and self-heating food dispensers. But most important of all was the directional radiation detector, which would locate and identify any potentially dangerous fissionable energy source in the glacier. Both Jamie and Arden were eager to set off, but Clent had insisted on the standard formality of departure briefing. Jamie stamped his feet impatiently as he spoke to the Doctor.

'Does he always have to do everything by the rule-book? Why doesn't he just wish us luck and let us get on with it!'

The Doctor shrugged. Clent was too complex a person to explain easily to someone as young and direct as Jamie.

'Forget about Clent, lad, and concentrate on being careful…' Then he added thoughtfully, 'Keep an eye on Arden, too. I don't think he quite realises how dangerous that creature is.'

Jamie knew that well enough, and wasn't afraid to admit it. 'After what happened in the laboratory, he must be blind then!'

'He is a scientist, after all,' murmured the Doctor, his eyes glinting mischievously. 'You know what they're like.' Jamie caught his glance, and chuckled, remembering what he'd had to put up with from the Doctor in the past.

'Aye! I know that all right!'

The briefing over, Arden was eager to leave. His enthusiasm bubbled over as Clent followed him through the airlock door.

'I hope we'll at least get a chance of taking a film of the warrior!' he blurted out boyishly. 'Mind you – we'll have to tread carefully. We don't know how many more of them will turn up.'

'I don't want you exposing yourself to unnecessary risks, Arden – remember that!' replied Clent crisply.

Arden paused and faced Clent, his face sober. 'Listen, Clent, we both know that I'm responsible for what's happened – as well as Davis's death. I'm not likely to be that stupid again, believe me!'

Clent didn't reply immediately. They both knew that if a dangerous power source *was* discovered in the glacier, Arden's archaeological adventure would in fact have saved Clent and the Base from complete annihilation. If the warrior had been left in the ice, no one would have been wise to the possible danger.

'Just get that information back to Base,' insisted Clent. 'And no desperate attempts to rescue the girl. She's the least of our worries.'

'Well I'm no leaving Victoria to that creature up there if there's half a chance of saving her!' snapped Jamie, who had heard the last remark.

'You will take your orders from Scientist Arden!' replied Clent, and disappeared through the door before Arden and Jamie had stepped into the airlock – and from there into the Arctic world outside. Once the temperature-sealed door had closed, even the Doctor couldn't hear the whine of the airsled as it skimmed across the snow towards the glacier. He turned and followed Clent back to the main building.

Clent was waiting for him in the corridor.

'Come along, Doctor,' he said genially. 'Time for you to show us what you can do.'

The Doctor forced a smile. He would much rather be with Jamie on the way to the ice face – but for now at least, his immediate purpose lay in unravelling the mystery of the Ioniser malfunction. It had to be prevented from happening again. 'By the way,' he asked, 'what was Penley working on when he left?'

The Doctor noted the effect of his question with interest. Clent glowered and looked the Doctor in the face. 'That information is top secret.' Turning on his heel, he brusquely led the way inside.

Storr thumped the table top angrily. 'A creature carved out of the ice! It's you that's been in a coma!'

'I'm telling you – it was real, and terrifying. And I'm not one for fairy stories – any more than you are. If I'd only seen it at the glacier, I'd agree with you. But it was inside the Base as well.'

Storr stared at him. 'Leave me out of your fun and games, then!' he growled. 'I've got enough to cope with.'

'You're certainly back to your old cheerful self,' said

Penley – and then stopped. 'What's the matter?'

Storr moved swiftly towards Penley, and whispered into his ear. 'Someone's outside. Not an animal – human. Trying to get in!'

'They must've tracked me back here from the Base. Quick – hide yourself. We don't want you carted off to Africa yet.'

In a second, Storr had hidden himself, and Penley was to all intents and purposes alone. Satisfied, he moved to boldly confront the intruder – and stepped back in surprise at the sight of Jan Garrett when he drew back the interior screen.

Penley's eyes glanced quickly behind Jan. She shook her head.

'It's all right – I'm alone.'

'Well, now you've followed me here, what do you want?' She had moved farther inside; the screen fell back across the doorway.

'Elric…' It was months now since anyone had called him by his first name. Jan had been his equal then; a genuine friend who showed some understanding of and sympathy for his clash with Clent – but not, he remembered bitterly, a fellow protester. Miss Garrett was too ambitious for that.

'You haven't forgotten my face then, Miss Garrett,' he said politely. He glanced at her lapel. 'No orders of merit yet? Not even for trying to cope with that stupid machine.'

'You're the only one who ever understood it,' she answered bluntly. 'We're in desperate trouble – help us!'

'Us? Does that include Clent?'

'He doesn't know I'm here.'

'I was going to say – he's the last person to need *me*!

All he needs is a mirror – preferably rose-tinted and of the magnifying sort.'

'He's ready to admit… that you have the knowledge he requires. He needs you – it's the only way he can be sure that the Ioniser will be permanently stabilised.'

'I'm surprised it hasn't already run wild, to tell the truth. Especially when I heard the evacuation broadcast. Some fluke saved him, I suppose?'

'A stranger came. He's eccentric – and infuriatingly like you. He doesn't think much of computers,' she added.

Penley smiled as he remembered the clownish intruder he'd met over Clent's unconscious body. 'Good for him!'

'But he doesn't know it all!' protested Jan. 'Only you know all the imperfections of Ioniser theory – even this stranger says it needs an expert!'

'And what does Clent say?'

'You know how proud he is. But his back's to the wall. Sooner or later he's going to have to make his report to the World Authority…'

'So sooner than have to admit failure, he'd like me back so he can produce a scapegoat! No thanks – let him face the music himself!'

'It was never easy. It's ten times worse now. Arden's made a fantastic discovery in the glacier.' She took a deep breath and stared at Penley. 'Aliens.'

To her surprise, Penley didn't even smile. He leant forward, his eyes keenly interested. 'Of course!' he exclaimed. 'It must be alien! That thing could never be an Earth hybrid or a throw-back!' He saw her look of surprise, and explained, 'I've seen it, you understand, at close range –

working at the ice face, blasting great chunks free!'

There was a small silence before Jan spoke again; this time her voice sounded strained. 'We think there may be an alien spaceship buried inside the ice,' continued Jan, 'and if it contains a nuclear power source…'

She didn't need to say any more. But Penley's brutal answer shook her.

'Then Clent's got no option, has he? He daren't use the Ioniser any more. He'll have to evacuate!'

Jan's anger flared. 'You know what's at stake! Five thousand years of civilisation! Clent won't give that up – none of us will! Even you can't deny what we're here for!' She paused, trying to control her anger. 'Doesn't our civilisation mean *anything* to you?'

'I know what it means to Clent!' replied Penley sharply. 'It's a computerised ant heap! Well I'm a man – not a machine! I'd sooner live with the Ice Age than with *his* sort of robot universe!'

He paused for breath. Jan took out her tranquilliser gun and pointed it straight at him. 'You must be desperate,' he remarked. 'But it'll do no good. You'll never manage to carry me even as far as your airsled.'

'I'm willing to try,' she said, then yelped with pain as Storr knocked the weapon sharply from her numbed hand. She turned, stared at Penley's savage-faced companion, and drew back nervously, holding her wrist. 'Who… are you?' she whispered.

'A friend,' said Penley, picking up the gun before Storr could reach it. 'You've said enough, Jan. Now leave us in peace. I'm not coming back with you – that's final.'

Storr turned on Penley. 'You're not letting her walk out of here just like that! Once she gets back there, she'll have this place swarming with security!' Desperate for a weapon, Storr snatched up a knife – but Penley's voice brought him to a halt.

'Storr – no!' The gun was pointing at Storr now. He dropped the knife back on to the table.

'It's the only way!'

'It's not my way – or yours,' replied Penley calmly, then switched his gaze to Jan. 'She won't give us away. I'm sure of that.'

'I give you my word…' Jan said quietly.

Storr turned away, disgusted by Penley's weakness. 'I don't trust any of them,' snarled the burly hunter, 'whatever they say!'

Penley pointed to the door with the gun. 'Return to Base, Miss Garrett.'

'And wait for Doomsday,' she murmured with a resigned shrug of her shoulders. She gave him one last look, then moved to the door while Penley held the screening skin to one side. For a brief moment they were out of earshot of Storr, and Penley took his opportunity quickly.

'If you still have trouble from the Ioniser,' he murmured, handing Jan back the gun, 'look up my notes on the Omega Factor. Good luck…'

He pushed her outside into the snow, and returned to the warmth of the stove. Storr was standing by it, his face unusually thoughtful.

'These aliens,' he brooded. 'They really exist, then…'

Penley was too preoccupied with his own thoughts to

wonder at the fact that Storr was expressing such interest in what was, after all, a scientific supposition.

'Yes,' declared Penley firmly, shrugging on his snow garments, 'and I intend to find out more about them.' With hardly a glance back, he shuffled quickly outside, and began his uphill trek to the glacier.

Somehow, Victoria had managed to snatch a few hours of fitful sleep. Every time she had woken up, Varga had been moving from one melting block of ice to the other, almost willing the creatures inside back to life… At dawn she awoke fully, and, shivering with cold, stared towards the glacier face in numb disbelief. Only two blocks of ice remained, and these were rapidly disintegrating as the creatures inside strove to break out – almost like dragon-men from monstrous frozen eggs, she thought. Their comrades stood around them, urging them into life with a chorus of hissing. Frightened yet fascinated, Victoria began to notice the differences between them: Varga's bearing and style of helmet and reptilian armour seemed of a superior nature to the others. He seemed to delegate more and more of the physical tasks to a second-in-command – whose name, Victoria gathered, was Zondal. He was just as gigantic in stature, but his whole aspect was fiercer and more repellent; and he snapped at and bullied the others. The remaining four warriors, including the two who had at last broken free of the ice, were less elegant and more clumsy than Varga, whose majestic bearing, seen in daylight, fitted all Victoria's ideas of a warlord. Zondal was harshly ordering the warriors into a simple formation, ready for inspection.

Varga turned and, seeing Victoria crouched and awake, strode over to her.

'You see?' He proudly gestured towards his warriors. 'It has worked! All my crew are alive! The ice is our friend!'

'Then you don't need me,' replied Victoria. 'Let me go back to my own people, please!'

The Martian warlord stared at her coldly. 'You will stay here with us,' he hissed. 'If you value your life, obey – and do not anger us!'

'But I'm no use to you!' protested Victoria. 'You don't need me – you have your warriors now.'

Ignoring this plea, Varga turned and summoned his second-in-command. 'Zondal!' As the warrior approached him and saluted in the Martian fashion – clenched fist to left shoulder – Varga continued, 'You will locate our buried spaceship without delay!'

'That will not be difficult, Commander,' came the harsh reply.

'You will then gain access to it by excavating into the glacier…' Varga paused. 'The cave that you will form will also act as an efficient trap. Proceed!'

Zondal saluted again, turned, and began to place his men at key points facing the glacier. Victoria had overheard Varga's strategy; her eyes were wide with alarm. 'But you don't need a trap. No one wants to attack you!' His grim face was implacable. She pleaded desperately. 'If you let them, they may be able to help you. You've only got to ask.'

The warlord looked down at her distraught face proudly. 'We do not need help. We are superior!'

Victoria protested, close to tears. 'You'd still be dead and frozen solid in there,' she cried out, pointing at the glacier, 'if it wasn't for us humans!'

'You are a child!' he sneered, then turned to watch Zondal organise the other warriors. Victoria wasn't going to be put off that easily.

'But what are you going to do with me?'

'A trap needs bait,' hissed the warlord. 'You will be the bait that draws your friends towards us.'

'No!' cried Victoria, in dismay. But there was no appeal against the cruel decision.

'Be silent!' ordered Varga. The violence in his voice quelled his prisoner completely. She huddled silently close to the snow crevasse, sullenly watching Zondal and his men.

At Varga's command, the sounding sensors on their breastplates glowed and pulsed – just as his own had done when he set out to locate his comrades. Zondal then strode forward, marked out a target area on the ice face, and gave the order.

'Sonic destructors at the ready!'

The four warriors raised their forearms in unison. The four tubular devices, pointed towards the target area.

'Set to wide impact,' Zondal paused briefly as his men made the necessary adjustments. 'Fire!'

The effect of the combined sonic weapons was devastating. The ice face crazed, shattered and erupted into fragments under the impact of the invisible beams, which clawed their way deeper and deeper into the heart of the glacier. Inside minutes, the once jagged mark on the ice had been gouged hollow – then it became a cave, and still later a massive crystalline cavern…

Victoria was not the only amazed observer. Hidden by an outcrop of frozen snow, Penley was taking in the scene from below. What the purpose of this task force was, he had no way of knowing – but they were armed, and had a human hostage! He looked towards the girl. Rescuing her was not going to be easy. Until the opportunity arose, he could only watch, and wait…

Clent stood in the doorway of the medicare laboratory, and nodded his head in disbelief. The area that had been assigned to the Doctor was no longer a neat and tidy desk unit – it was almost buried under an untidy mountain of torn and crumpled paper. And the Doctor – totally unaware of Clent's presence – was on his knees, searching desperately for the vital scrap of calculation… Clent moved forward until he was standing almost directly in front of the scavenging Doctor. But he still wasn't noticed – until the Doctor came to the particular piece of paper that Clent was standing on. 'Excuse me…' he murmured, and snatched it up. Suddenly his face broke into a broad grin. 'Ah! I thought so! Of course! Reverse the sequence and it gives a density ratio to the power of ten!' he exclaimed gleefully, throwing his arms into the air and discarding the items that he had just been grovelling for so diligently – and at the same time seeing Clent for the first time.

'Genius at work, I see,' remarked the Base Leader drily. 'Wouldn't it be simpler if you used our computer?'

The Doctor paused in his frantic scurrying about, and, catching sight of a marker scribe in Clent's lapel, snatched it with a smile.

'Just the thing!' he exclaimed, and started writing an extended series of calculations at shoulder height all along the nearest bare wall. Suddenly the Doctor stopped, bit his lip thoughtfully, and shook his head. 'It's not right!' he muttered. 'Something's missing!'

At that moment, Jan Garrett entered, carrying a small sheaf of notes. She handed them to the Doctor. He took them eagerly.

'Your instructions were to help the Doctor, Miss Garrett,' said Clent coldly. 'Where have you been?'

'Obtaining these notes from Scientist Penley's file.'

'You had no authority—' Clent ranted. But the Doctor cut short his angry reaction with a cry of triumph.

'That's it!' he blurted out, elated. 'The Omega factor! Clever chap, your friend Penley. Why did you ever get rid of him?'

Clent was too preoccupied with checking the formula to react to this sharp observation. As he reached the final equation, his face smiled in admiration and pride.

'It's amazing! And it was staring us in the face all the time…'

Jan hadn't the same theoretical training as Clent or Penley. She had been trained to rely on the computer for formula analysis. 'Will it work?' she asked Clent anxiously.

Clent quickly copied down the essential numbers. 'I'll run it through the computer myself!' the Leader exclaimed, and hurried out, followed by Jan and the Doctor. The Doctor, turning to Jan, sighed and shook his head disapprovingly.

'It doesn't need running through a computer,' he complained, 'it's perfect!' He glanced mischievously at Jan, as they hurried along the corridor leading to the control room and the computer. 'I deserve an apology,' he said, and then added, 'Penley, too. Thank you for digging out his notes.'

'I thought they might help...' murmured Jan, leading the way across to ECCO, where Clent was studying the computer print-out. He was completely absorbed, his eyes glued to the machine. He made no sign of hearing the ensuing exchange between the Doctor and Jan.

'Pity Penley turned traitor...' remarked the Doctor innocently. Jan's reaction was immediate, and angry.

'He was *not* a traitor! He's the most brilliant scientist we have, and if you—'

The Doctor cut her short and smiled gently. 'I'm glad he's still got some friends here at Base. I needed to know—'

'It works!' cried Clent. 'The computer says it works!'

Suddenly, the static-distorted voice of Arden crackled out from the video-communicator. The geologist's hooded face showed fuzzily on the videoscreen, and he spoke urgently.

'Glacier Task Unit to Base,' he called, 'Arden to Leader Clent. Over, over!'

Clent moved quickly to establish contact. 'Clent here, Arden. Report.'

'We've arrived at the glacier site...' Arden's words faded in a sudden rush of static, then cleared again. 'There's something strange here. Can you hear me?'

'Bad atmospherics,' replied Clent, emphasising his words for clarity. 'You'll have to speak up. We'll try and boost you...' He waved a vague hand towards Jan, and she tried to adjust the controls.

'What has he found?' asked the Doctor impatiently.

'The ice face,' crackled Arden's disembodied voice. 'It's been excavated… into a sort of cave.'

'Excavated?' queried Clent.

'How?' demanded the Doctor tensely.

'Not a drill,' replied Arden, 'nor explosives… some sort of power tool, I'd say.'

'Is there any sign of a spacecraft?' demanded Clent.

Arden's blunt answer brought them all forward, tense and expectant.

'Yes… at the back of… the excavation… there's what looks like – a metal door!'

Clent looked first at Jan, and then at the Doctor. The spacecraft theory was right – but would its propulsion unit bring the danger that they feared?

'The place seems deserted…' Arden continued. 'But the Ice Warrior couldn't have done this… alone.'

'Don't get any closer than you need,' warned the Doctor.

'Arden, get those radiation readings quickly – and come back here at the double! Don't take any chances!'

For once, Arden didn't need Clent's warning. He shuddered as he began to set up the radiation detector, apprehension mingling with the enjoyment of discovery. Jamie looked about, but he could see no sign of the warrior, or that Victoria had ever been here…

'We'll take the readings first, Jamie…' murmured Arden, 'and then we'll have a look round outside for Victoria. All right?' He gave the Scots lad a quick smile.

'Fair enough,' agreed Jamie. He knew the importance of the mission Clent had ordered; but he was glad that Arden shared his own feelings about Victoria.

'What readings are these, then?' he asked, as they unwound the power pack connections.

'Radiation – magnetic field – ion density... it won't take long.'

'Just as well,' muttered Jamie. 'I don't much like this place – nor that door.' He stared at it, frowning. 'I wonder what's inside it?'

Arden threw him a quick, amused glance. 'You don't think I'm leaving here until I've had a go at opening it, do you? There's never been a discovery like this before—'

They were the last words he ever spoke. At Varga's silent command, the warriors stepped out of hiding and opened fire. Victoria, her mouth smothered by Varga's mighty fist, could only watch in helpless terror as Arden took the full brunt of the massive burst of sonic power. His body seemed to shimmer, almost disintegrate, beneath the invisible blast of energy. For a split second, he seemed suspended like a broken puppet, his face crumpled in agonised surprise. Then he slumped to the ground beside Jamie, as though hurled there by a giant hand. The ambush complete, Varga released the girl. She stood trembling, staring at the two sprawled bodies on the cavern floor, her face wide-eyed with misery. 'You've... killed them!'

6

Under the Moving Mountain

The Doctor prowled round the Ioniser Room like a caged animal, his puckish features clearly showing his deep anxiety. Since completing the Ionisation formula, he'd been able to think of nothing but Victoria – and now nearly an hour had passed since Arden and Jamie had last made contact.

The Doctor paused before the video-communicator. He was just about to operate it, when Clent strode into the room, bursting with elation at the compliments showered on him by the World Scientific Director. Seeing the Doctor's intention, he moved forward and intercepted his hand at the video controls, and questioned him with a frown.

'What are you doing?'

'I'm worried. Arden and Jamie should've reported in again by now!'

'You know what Arden is like,' he replied cheerfully – 'full of scientific curiosity…'

'I think we should find out,' suggested the Doctor, again reaching for the video.

'If you don't mind,' replied Clent, reaching the controls first, 'I'll handle this.' He adjusted the controls and spoke crisply into the machine. 'Base to Glacier Task Force –

Leader Clent calling Scientist Arden. Arden, do you read me!'

There was no response other than the harsh surge of static. The videoscreen was blank. Clent frowned, and spoke again more brusquely. 'Arden – answer me! Arden!'

The Doctor's mouth tightened. 'Something *is* wrong...' he muttered. 'I'll never forgive myself if anything's happened to those two youngsters.'

Jan entered briskly, still smiling from Clent's achievement. Her face fell when she saw the two men staring anxiously at the faintly nickering videoscreen. 'What's wrong?' she asked.

'No reply from Arden.' Clent tried to brighten the gloom. 'At least we've made the breakthrough with the Ioniser!' He beamed at the Doctor. 'The World Director assured me that there'll be suitable... recognition for all the members of our little group! We've got that machine under complete control at last!' But his face fell at the Doctor's reply.

'What a pity we shan't be able to use it then.'

Clent and Miss Garrett looked at him blankly for a moment – then the truth of his statement sunk in.

'You're forgetting that Arden hasn't yet completed his mission,' the Doctor continued. 'And until we know the facts about that alien spaceship, we daren't go on!'

Penley had watched the ambush in the ice cave with horror. Minutes after the aliens had retreated into the doorway in the ice, dragging the girl with them, he had managed to pull himself together enough to scurry silently across to the two crumpled bodies. To his astonishment, he had found that Jamie, partly protected from the warriors' deadly fire-power by Arden's body, was still alive! Summoning up the strength to drag the lad's limp form to the waiting airsled, he had brought him back to Storr's hideout. He could do nothing to save the girl – but as he sped back to safety, his mind raced. What was behind the door in the ice?

Storr's immediate reaction to Jamie was predictable and fierce. 'Why bring him back here?' he growled. 'Another mouth to feed.' But he changed his tune when Penley showed him the spoils he had brought on the airsled: food, a first-aid kit, and sleeping bags. He listened, frowning, to Penley's description of the cave and the door set into the ice.

'It has to be a spacecraft of some kind! And big enough to hold six of those hulking brutes – as well as the girl!'

Suddenly, Jamie groaned, and half-opened his bloodshot eyes. 'Where... am I?' he whispered hoarsely.

'Never you mind,' growled Storr. 'Somewhere safe...'

'You're suffering from severe shock, lad,' soothed Penley. 'Take it easy.'

'What happened? Where's Arden?' Jamie's eyes flicked nervously from Storr to Penley.

'Dead,' replied Penley quietly. 'You were both shot down by the warriors. He got the worst of it.' He frowned, remembering that horrific moment. 'Some sort of ray gun, I'd say.'

'So we failed then...' Jamie murmured bitterly.

'Came to rescue the girl – is that it?' demanded Storr.

Jamie tried to sit up, his eyes bright. 'Have ye seen Victoria? Is she alive?'

The effort was too much and he fell back – but Penley's words eased the pain. 'Yes, she's alive all right – but you just take it easy, lad.' His face looked grave. 'She's a prisoner.'

'Then we've got to save her!' exclaimed Jamie. 'Help me – please!' He began to slip back into unconsciousness.

'We'll discuss it later,' soothed Penley.

Storr looked from the prostrate boy to Penley, who shook his head solemnly.

'I don't know what his chances are, Storr,' remarked the scientist. 'As for the girl…' He looked down at Jamie sadly, 'there's nothing *we* can do…'

Inside the spaceship, Victoria was waiting for her opportunity. Although still feigning unconsciousness, she was now sharply alert and determined to escape. She had to know if Jamie was alive or dead – and somehow she had to let the Doctor know about the aliens and the plan she had overheard them discussing earlier.

'Will there be more Earthlings, Commander?' Zondal had asked, obviously only too ready to kill again.

'Not yet,' Varga had replied. 'If more come, we know we can destroy them. If no others seek this girl, then we know they are too few to resist us.'

'Let us kill her now. It will make no difference!'

'No! We may need her voice to lure them here.' The majestic head had nodded towards the complex machinery. 'You have a more urgent task, Zondal: the propulsion unit – we need it to break free of the ice.'

The warlord had then held up the portable power pack he had removed from the radiation detector unit outside after killing Arden. 'This may help us,' he hissed, and strode across to the compact machine section out of Victoria's line of vision.

Now, at last, she was alone. All the other warriors were preparing the spaceship for action – and the way to the airlock was clear. As long as she remembered how to work the controls! Stealthily, she crept towards the door. Her hand brushed the sensor control. With the faintest of whispers, the door opened, then shut automatically after her. Inside the airlock, she quickly found the outer door control. At her touch, it opened – and she was free!

But her immediate plan was to find Jamie. She ran to where he and Arden had fallen – and froze in shock and amazement. Jamie was gone! Her face softened at the sight of the geologist's body – but she had no time to lose. With a simple gesture, she covered the dead man's face, then looked wildly about her. Jamie couldn't have been killed after all – but he might well be injured or severely wounded. She had to find him! But she saw the deep grooves in the snow – as if a heavy object had been dragged away – perhaps by a wild animal, she speculated with a shudder.

Just then her eye fell on Arden's dead wrist, and her heart jumped. His wrist-video! If she could only make it work! It could make contact with the Base – and the Doctor! With a silent apology to the dead man for the necessary theft, she quickly eased the device from his already stiffening arm. Scurrying into the shelter of a spur of ice that hid her from the Martian spacecraft, she studied the tiny controls. To her delight, there was only one – the device must be pre-set.

'Doctor – Leader Clent – Miss Garrett!' she cried in an urgent whisper. 'This is Victoria! Please – somebody answer me!'

She wasn't to know that her every move was being watched by Varga and Zondal on the spaceship's video system, and that even her whispered call for help was being picked up and relayed clearly to the vigilant warlord. He laughed coldly.

'The girl has courage,' he hissed, 'but she is stupid to think that we would not watch her every move.'

'She will betray us, Commander!' declared Zondal. He pointed to the sonic cannon that could operate from the side of the ship at the touch of the button beneath his cruel fist. 'She must be destroyed!'

'No, Zondal,' ordered the warlord. 'Let her talk first. There are things we need to know.'

Just as Victoria was about to give up in tearful frustration, a small burst of sound came from the tiny communicator. The familiar face of the Doctor appeared on its screen.

'Victoria! Where are you?' he asked frantically. 'Are you all right? Where's Jamie – and Arden?'

Gulping back the tears that threatened to overcome her, Victoria briefly described the situation. 'I don't know where Jamie is – but Arden is dead!' She took a deep breath, trying to thrust that terrifying memory from her mind. 'It was the Ice Warriors. They have a terrible weapon – a sort of ray gun.' Her voice began to rise hysterically; she tried desperately to control her shaking hands. 'Doctor – they're from Mars! They're vicious – ruthless!'

Clent's cool voice cut across her panic, and brought her

under control once more. 'Keep calm, girl!' he rapped. 'We must have facts! Tell us about the spaceship! Quickly!'

A sudden wave of anger swept over Victoria. She almost shouted at the calm face which stared back at her from the tiny video. 'Don't you understand? They've killed Arden, and Jamie's disappeared! Don't you even care?'

'Of course we care, Victoria,' came the Doctor's gentle reply. 'But we need to know something about that spaceship's propulsion unit – it's vital.'

'Propulsion unit?' queried Victoria blankly.

Clent's face reappeared; his voice was sharp. 'Engines, girl – engines!'

'Oh, I see…' answered Victoria tiredly. 'I think they're repairing the engines now.'

'What kind are they?' demanded Clent urgently. 'Reactor turbine – ion jet – anti-gravity? Think, girl!'

Before Victoria could answer, a mighty shudder shook the ground, bringing a flurry of ice down from the excavated ceiling, and knocking Victoria breathless to the floor.

'Victoria – what's happening?' came the Doctor's voice. 'Are you all right?'

'Yes, I'm all right, Doctor…' she replied. 'It's the glacier – we're right inside it, and it's moving all the time!'

'The engines, Victoria—' broke in Clent's demanding tones, 'for heaven's sake, tell us about the engines!'

'Give me a chance!' protested Victoria. 'I'm trying to think!'

But Varga had heard enough. With a curt gesture, he ordered one of the warriors to the airlock door.

'She must say no more. Turoc, bring the girl in here – quickly!'

Zondal turned to his commander. 'It would be easier – and quicker – to kill her now.'

'You do not understand, Zondal,' breathed Varga harshly. 'There are questions she must answer! Why are the Earthlings so interested in our engines? Why are they afraid?' He turned away from the viewing screen for a moment and looked thoughtfully back towards the engine room. 'We must have these answers, Zondal,' he hissed – 'and quickly!'

In that brief moment, if he or Zondal had been watching, they would have seen Victoria's tense reaction to the opening of the door in the ice. She spoke quickly into the communicator, and prepared to make her escape. 'There's someone coming from the spaceship. I'm going to have to run for it!'

'Try to get back to Base, Victoria!' urged the Doctor – but Victoria was no longer listening. With a tightening of her throat, she realised that the Ice Warrior now standing in the open airlock was cutting off her escape route out of the cave and down the hillside to the Base. Turoc paused and, turning in a slow arc, activated his radar detector. As it started to pulse, Victoria looked desperately about her and, without further hesitation, took her only escape route – through the tunnels that led deeper into the glacier...

Turoc had not seen her swift escape from the cave – but his finding device registered an alien presence moving through the maze of ice grottoes beyond the spaceship. He followed with great crushing strides, smashing his way into the main tunnel, the finding device guiding him relentlessly on. Ahead of him, running and clambering desperately over the debris of fallen ice, Victoria looked for an escape route that would take her out of the mountain of ice and into the open snow. But whichever way she turned, the Ice Warrior was behind her, driving her further and further into the heart of the glacier. She stumbled; her heart sank. There was no escape – she was trapped!

Clent turned bitterly away from the blank screen, and ground his fist into the palm of his hand. 'It's hopeless! We know nothing! We're helpless!' He turned on the Doctor, who was dialling a chemical formula on the automatic dispenser. 'What on earth are you doing? There's no time for playthings!'

'The position isn't good, I agree,' mused the Doctor. 'Jamie has vanished. Victoria is on the run. And we still don't know anything useful about that spacecraft's propulsion unit, do we?' The machine delivered two small phials into his waiting hand. He smiled. 'Perhaps this will help.'

'Ammonium sulphide?' asked Clent in astonishment. 'You're crazy!'

'Am I really? Think a moment, will you? We know these aliens are from Mars. What do we know of their planet's atmospheric conditions? Mmm?'

It was Jan who answered, just as puzzled as Clent. 'It's chiefly nitrogen, with virtually no oxygen or hydrogen.'

'So they wouldn't enjoy sniffing this little mixture, would they?'

Clent looked intrigued, though not convinced. 'You

don't mean you're going to use this stuff as a form of toxic gas!' He paused. 'And anyway, how do you propose to get it to them?'

'I'll take it myself. Oh, I'm aware we've lost Arden already – but I know what to expect, remember. He didn't.' He smiled at the two innocent-looking phials, one in each hand. 'That's why I'm going prepared.'

Clent glared at him furiously. 'I refuse to let you go! I dare not lose any more personnel!'

'My dear chap, I'm not even on your pay roll. The Ioniser will work very well without me – and after all, *someone* has to identify that alien propulsion unit, don't they?' He paused and grinned. 'Who better than me?'

'Very well, Doctor – on your own head be it. I agree – but strictly under protest!'

'Thank you. I hoped you'd see it my way; Now – a small matter of communication!'

Jan produced a wrist-video, demonstrating it as she strapped it on to the Doctor's wrist. 'This is identical to the one that Victoria was using,' she explained.

Clent looked amazed. 'Is that all you're taking?' he gasped, indicating the wrist-video and the two phials.

'There's nothing else I need, is there?' replied the Doctor innocently. 'What do you suggest?'

'Weapons, man!' Clent exclaimed. 'Those warriors are armed!'

'But I'm not going there to fight a duel. That isn't what I've got in mind at all.'

Clent stared at him blankly. What was this ridiculous man up to now? As though the question had been asked aloud, the Doctor promptly supplied the answer.

'I'm going to let them take me prisoner.'

Somehow Victoria had managed to evade the oncoming
Ice Warrior by scrambling through openings so small that
the alien couldn't follow her – but he had simply broken his
way through the ice walls, blindly following the quickening
sonic pulse. The heart of the glacier seemed like a gigantic
maze, twisting and turning upon itself, perforated with
crystalline hollows and pockets, chimneys and tunnels.
Suddenly forced into what looked like a cul-de-sac, Victoria
looked about her desperately. There was only one way out:
through a narrow crevice which was scarcely wide enough
to take her body. But the ice was so thick that even the
massive Turoc would take hours to break it down – time
enough for her to escape!

She had almost succeeded in wriggling through, feet first,
when she heard the crushing approach of the Ice Warrior!
Panicking, she dropped the precious communicator – her
only link with the Base, and human help. She knew that
she must have the device – without it she would be utterly
lost. It lay on the floor only a yard away. Stretching back
through the crevice, she could almost reach it – the effort
wracked her weary muscles to breaking point; the ice
became a living creature, creaking and groaning all around
her. And beyond the rumbling menace of the ice, she could
hear the steady, crunching tread of Turoc's feet – and the
menacing hiss of his approaching breath.

Abandoning the struggle to reach the communicator,
Victoria tried to draw back out of his reach – but she was

stuck! With horror, she realised that she couldn't move! Then, just as the Ice Warrior's massive fist clamped down on her wrist, there came a shudder and a roar of moving ice! The body of the Ice Warrior was crushed by the ceiling of the tunnel as it fell in on top of him! When the moment of terror had passed, and the eerie silence returned, Victoria suddenly realised that the grip of the crevice round her body had loosened – she could move! Now was her chance of escape – before another movement of the glacier brought down an avalanche of ice on top of her, too! And then she discovered the grim truth: her puny strength couldn't budge the grip of Turoc's mighty fist – even in death he held her a prisoner in the heart of the moving mountain of ice!

7

Diplomat in Danger

'His fever's gone,' observed Storr brusquely, looking down at Jamie's sleeping body. 'His body's young. It'll soon heal.'

'Yes, of course it will,' replied Penley, but he didn't sound convinced.

'What are you worried about then?'

Penley frowned, remembering the Ice Warriors' vicious attack. 'The weapons they used…' he brooded, 'peculiar…' He snapped out of his thoughts and faced Storr squarely. 'The fact is I'm afraid there might be some neural damage. He has no reflex response from the waist down.'

Storr had seen spinal paralysis in animals and men before; the only hope of survival would be intensive care and proper treatment. Was this an excuse for Penley to return to the Base? 'How can you be sure, if he's unconscious?'

'I'm not – yet. When he wakes, and tries to walk – then we'll know.'

'And if it's bad?'

'I'll have to get him to the Base,' he said bluntly.

'No!' cried Storr fiercely.

'For the boy's sake! Do you want him to end up a cripple?'

Storr fell silent. He knew the other answer wasn't easy,

but his hatred of the scientists and their degrading power forced him to make the suggestion. 'There's another way to save him – to befriend the aliens!'

Penley stared at him in disbelief. 'Don't be a fool! They're ruthless warriors, trained to kill!'

'In self defence!' growled Storr. 'I know what it's like, remember? If their weapons did this to the boy, they'll know both cause and cure – it's obvious.'

'What makes you think you can talk to them?' demanded Penley. 'They killed Arden!'

'They were afraid! You said yourself that he'd set up some scientific gear or other – they probably thought he was going to attack them! Why shouldn't they defend themselves? *I* would!'

'But the boy isn't one of their kind!' Penley replied. 'He's human – one of us!'

'When I explain that he's not a scientist, they'll understand.'

'Wait!' Penley cried. 'At least try to—'

He never completed the sentence. A single brutal blow from Storr's encased arm knocked him to the ground unconscious. Storr crouched by him long enough to make sure the damage was only temporary. Grunting, 'Peace at last' he began his preparations for the journey to the glacier.

In the engine room of the spaceship, Zondal was making a critical report to his commander.

'All fuel has degenerated beyond use,' the lieutenant stated grimly – 'including emergency reserves.'

'That would normally take thousands of years,' whispered Varga. 'The Earthlings were right.'

'Without fuel, we are helpless!' exclaimed Zondal. 'We will never be able to break free from the ice!'

'Is that what they fear, Zondal?' the Martian warlord queried. 'That our energy source could explode? If that is so – if they understand such physical principles – they may have developed a similar form of reactor!'

'And they will have the fuel elements we need!' agreed Zondal eagerly. 'They must be made to give the fuel to us!'

'That is where the girl will be of use,' replied Varga. 'She will give us information, and help us bargain for our needs…'

'But she has not been found. Turoc has not yet returned.'

'We have no time to waste,' rasped his commander. 'We must make other plans.' He looked through into the control room, and made an instant decision. 'Zondal' – he commanded – 'unship the sonic cannon!' The cruel laughter coughed from his armoured throat. 'The Earthlings will not argue with that!'

Outside the excavated cave, Storr paused in amazement. To tear a whole cave out of the guts of the glacier – that had taken some doing! He moved forward stealthily until he was inside the cave and within sight of the metal door. The place was deserted. Skirting its perimeter he paused in a side cave, struggling to think of the best way to make contact – he didn't intend falling into a trap laid for visiting scientists!

Suddenly, he heard a distant, plaintive voice, human and female, crying for help! As the faint cry was repeated, he realised that it wasn't coming from the metal door, or from the main cave itself, but from within the glacier. Catching sight of a tunnel-like gap in the darkest shadows of the cave in which he was standing, he moved towards its entrance and listened again. Yes, it was a woman's voice – a girl's!

'Help…!' came a desperate cry. 'Help me…!'

It was unlikely to be a trap, set so far away from the alien's spaceship, and the cry itself sounded genuine enough. Besides, if it was the girl, perhaps she could tell him more about these unearthly creatures, before he confronted them. The glacier shuddered, and he saw he'd have to act quickly. Dodging the fragments of ice that fell spasmodically, he hurried towards the calling voice.

The sound was closer now; and as Storr emerged into a tunnel almost filled with ice debris, he saw Victoria, gesturing towards her wrist. Clamped round it was a metallic fist, which was holding her prisoner! As more fragments of ice rained upon them, Storr worked quickly to force the alien's iron grip apart. Victoria looked at him hopefully.

'Can you get me free?' she pleaded.

'What happened?' Storr was finding the job more difficult than he thought, with only one arm in use.

'I ran away,' explained Victoria. 'He'd just grabbed me when the roof fell, and crushed him.'

Storr flicked a puzzled glance at the girl's face. 'Why run away?'

It was Victoria's turn to look surprised. 'The warriors – they're evil!' she exclaimed. 'They killed Arden – they want to destroy the Base, too, I think!'

Storr paused, suddenly interested. 'They're against the scientists then!'

'I tried to tell them about the Ioniser – but they seem to think that it's some kind of weapon of destruction!' Storr's eyes turned fiercely upon her.

'That's just what it is!' he growled. 'It'll destroy the whole of civilisation!' His face was fanatical.

'But the Ioniser is meant to hold back the ice!'

The ragged pirate gave her a fierce glance, then pulled her free of the crevasse and the Ice Warrior.

'Come on,' he said, leading the way back to the main cave. 'We've got no time to lose!'

Victoria pulled at his arm, urgently. 'Not that way!' she cried. 'The Ice Warriors—!'

'You want to help your young friend, don't you?' demanded Storr. Victoria stared at him, then almost laughed with relief.

'Jamie?' she cried. 'You know where he is? Is he hurt?'

Her face fell at Storr's reply.

'He's desperately ill. I was going for help when I heard you—'

'Help?' asked Victoria, confused. 'Here?'

'From the aliens in that spaceship,' Storr told her, then, seeing her fear, went on. 'We'll be all right – they'll listen to me. I'm against the scientists, like they are – so we've got something in common for a start!'

'You don't know what you're doing!' cried Victoria, trying to draw back. 'No – I won't go to them! They'll kill me!'

Storr was in no mood for argument. Grasping Victoria's arm, he bundled her brutally along the ice tunnel, and away from the imminent avalanche. 'They're against Clent and his sort and the Ioniser – that's good enough for me!' he growled. 'And if you stay here, you'll die anyway! Come on!'

Victoria followed Storr out to the safety of the main cavern. But there they stopped – abruptly. Facing them, guns at the ready, were Varga and his warriors – and they looked anything but friendly. Storr, seeing them for the first time, at last understood why Penley and Victoria had been afraid. Fearsome brutes, no doubt about that – but what allies they would make against the scientists! Varga stepped closer to Victoria and spoke, his voice harsh.

'Where is Turoc?' he demanded.

Aware how close she and Storr were to death, Victoria answered weakly, 'He was crushed to death... by the ice.' She sensed Varga's rising anger, and quailed before it. 'It wasn't my fault!' she cried.

'I gave you your life,' the warlord hissed venomously, 'but you ran away. Because of that, one of my men is dead!' He gestured to Isbur, the warrior closest to the girl. 'Take her inside!'

Victoria didn't resist – there was no point. But as she entered the spaceship's gleaming airlock, Isbur's fist upon her arm, she threw Storr one last anguished look.

With a broad smile, Storr extended his hand to the Ice Warrior. The gesture was ignored.

'Identify yourself!' rasped the alien leader.

'My name's Storr,' stated the hunter pleasantly. 'I'm a scavenger – a Loyalist!'

118

Varga was interested – Storr could see that. 'You are from the Base?' the Martian whispered keenly.

'No fear! I'm against the scientists! They're devils, the lot of them!'

'Then you know nothing of their machines?'

'I don't want to! They're out to destroy our world – and I want to help you destroy *them*! I'm on your side!'

It was Zondal who spoke now, as Varga lost interest. 'What good are you to us?'

'I know the land here – lived here all my life. I can help you!' But he had seen Varga's chilling response, and knew the truth at last.

'You are not a scientist…' uttered the warlord, coldly, 'therefore you are useless and unnecessary.' He gave a nod – and Storr crumpled before him, scythed down by the sonic guns.

'Now to question the girl…' Varga whispered hoarsely, and turned back towards the spaceship.

Clent turned from studying the Ioniser monitors to find Miss Garrett standing at his shoulder. Her face was tense as she passed him a seismic print-out. 'The glacier is moving again!'

Clent drew in a sharp breath. 'The fifth surge today,' he exclaimed, and moved across to the electronic wall chart that marked the glacier's grim progress. 'The Ioniser isn't holding it…'

'We're down to half power,' Jan pointed out nervously. 'We daren't go above that level…'

Clent's features tightened with anger. 'If only we

knew what was inside that spaceship. Until we do, we're helpless!'

Because of the one missing factor, they couldn't put their problem to ECCO, the all-knowing computer; Clent had not even notified World Control – for him, an unprecedented omission.

'We must decide soon,' insisted Jan.

'Not until we know the facts, Miss Garrett!'

'Supposing the Doctor fails?' she demanded. 'Suppose we never find out?'

'We'll face that when we have to.'

'But we must be prepared! There has to be a contingency plan if everything else goes wrong!'

Clent looked at Jan dispassionately. 'Nothing will go wrong. The Doctor will succeed. He *has* to!'

When the Doctor at last reached the ice cavern, he found Penley crouched over Storr's dead body. After a moment's pause, Penley covered the lifeless face for the last time.

Penley attempted to explain. 'Storr came up here to talk to the aliens. He thought they'd be able to do some good for the youngster I found here.'

'Jamie?' asked the Doctor eagerly. 'You know where he is? And what about the girl – Victoria?'

Penley threw a brief glance at the spaceship door. 'She must still be inside there with them. The lad's back at our hideout. I think he'll be all right, but...' His voice trailed away sadly.

The Doctor looked at him soberly. 'Better let me know the worst. Is it bad?'

'He must've been shot by the alien ray guns. There may be some spinal damage – paralysis.'

The Doctor looked grim. 'Then there's only one place for him, isn't there?'

Penley nodded. 'The medicare centre at Base…'

'Take my airsled,' the Doctor said firmly. 'Get Jamie on to it and take him back there – if it's as bad as you say.'

'It's his only hope.'

He lurched against the Doctor as the icy ground shuddered beneath them. 'The glacier's moving,' observed the Doctor.

'It's getting worse,' agreed Penley. 'Let's get out of here!'

'You carry on,' came the reply, 'I've got a job to do.'

Penley nodded towards the spaceship door. 'In there?'

The Doctor nodded. 'There's Victoria, for one thing – and for another, Clent has to know whether the alien reactor unit will explode if the Ioniser is used properly.' As Penley stared at him in surprise, the Doctor smiled, 'I adapted your notes on the Omega Factor.'

'Did you now…' murmured Penley, with new respect.

'But you're the chap to handle it,' insisted the Doctor. 'Do you think you can cope with Clent?'

'I dare say I can manage to stay sane.' He looked down at Storr's body. 'I'll take Storr back to his hideout with me. He'd've preferred it there.'

With that, he dragged his friend to the Doctor's airsled.

When Penley was well clear of the glacier, the Doctor activated the tiny communicator. 'Doctor to Clent,' he called. 'I'm going in now, old chap. Wish me luck.' Then he tucked the device away.

With that, he moved boldly towards the sleek metallic door, and hammered on it with his fist.

'Open this door at once!' he demanded brazenly. 'Open up, I say!' To his surprise, the door opened immediately, and he stepped inside the airlock. It closed behind him, and he waited for the inner door to open – but it did not. Instead, a harsh voice spoke from a loudspeaker set in the ceiling panel.

'Identify yourself!'

The Doctor spoke sternly. 'I am a diplomatic messenger. I don't answer questions until I am properly received by a suitable person!'

'You will answer now!' snapped the voice. The Doctor folded his arms, tilted his chin up defiantly, and remained silent.

'Unless you answer inside ten seconds,' the voice continued, 'the atmospheric pressure will be reduced to zero – a perfect vacuum.'

The Doctor's face filled with alarm.

'In that condition, your Earthling body will explode. Countdown commences now. Ten… nine… eight…'

The Doctor's eyes found the atmospheric level indicator by his side – the pressure was decreasing fast!

'If you insist,' he shouted acidly. 'But I don't think much of your hospitality!' The pressure gauge sank lower. 'I'm a scientist – from the Base – I want to help you!' The level stopped sinking, and, a second later, it rose to normal. The inner door slid open, and the Doctor found himself confronted by the Martian warlord inside the spaceship. Flanking him were several other Ice Warriors.

'You are a scientist?' queried Varga coldly. 'You do not look like one!' he gazed at the Doctor's eccentric dress.

'He looks more like the human we destroyed – the scavenger,' remarked Zondal sourly. 'He could be an imposter. We should destroy him also!'

'If you kill me, you'll ruin any chance you might have of escape! Or perhaps you intend to stay inside this glacier permanently.'

Varga stepped forward arrogantly. 'I am Varga, the Martian warlord. Explain how you can help us!'

'There are certain conditions that have to be met first,' insisted the Doctor.

'You are our prisoner!' hissed the warlord furiously. 'It is I who set conditions and ask questions!'

The Doctor held up his hand, and smiled. 'Listen!' The faintest of tremors ran through the spaceship. Its sound sensors were picking up the creak and grind of the ice mountain outside. 'It is you who are the prisoners,' the Doctor pointed out gently, '… and I who can set you free!'

'On *my* terms!' snarled the warlord. He gestured to Isbur. 'Bring the girl!' Turning back to the Doctor, he continued. 'Now we have two hostages, *we* make the bargains here!'

'You haven't got time to bargain – before long, the glacier will crush and destroy you and your ship! But we have a device that can melt the ice and release you!'

'We know of this device,' hissed Varga. 'The girl has told us its name – the Ioniser.' His voice changed to bitter anger. 'Do not try to trick us! We know it is a weapon aimed to

123

destroy us!'

Before the Doctor could answer this charge, Victoria was led in by Isbur. When she saw the Doctor, her face fell. 'Oh, Doctor, they've got you too!'

'Don't worry, Victoria, we're not beaten yet.' He smiled cheerfully. 'Jamie's safe and well, for a start!'

Victoria's face flooded with relief and hope, but Varga's harsh whisper brought the Doctor back to the nub of the matter.

'If what you say is true, why have you not freed us before?'

The Doctor's eye flicked beyond the Martian to what looked like a complex technical area. Could it be the engine room? Somehow he had to find out without giving his hand away! He hesitated. 'Er… there are certain difficulties.'

But the Doctor's probing glance had confirmed the Warlord's suspicions. 'You are afraid of us!' he exclaimed keenly. 'You are afraid our ship will explode!'

The Doctor tried to put the problem simply. 'If the Ioniser causes a nuclear holocaust, it'll defeat its original purpose – to hold back the glaciers!'

'That is what I suspected…' breathed the warlord; and then gave that peculiar choking laugh that so often meant danger. 'You dare not act against us!'

'We don't want to harm you, or your ship,' repeated the Doctor irritably. 'I keep telling you, our action would release it – you'd be free!'

'But if the ice melted too quickly,' Zondal pointed out, 'there would be severe flooding.'

'And our engines would be useless!' hissed Varga. 'We

would be at your mercy – and there would be *no* escape!'

'You can walk out of here now,' suggested the Doctor. 'You'd be safe – even if your spacecraft *was* destroyed.'

'But without this vehicle,' whispered the grim-faced warlord, 'we cannot return to our planet.'

The Doctor was about to inform the Ice Warrior that his distant home planet – Mars – had long since died, when he stopped himself, horrified. With nowhere to return to, the Martians would be forced to stay – but it wasn't in their nature to remain guests for long. They were conquerors, colonisers and invaders; and with their deadly weapons, probably invincible! Suddenly, the Doctor thought of a vital question. 'Why did you come here in the first place? What was your mission, Varga. Tell me!'

'To investigate this planet… and report,' answered Varga. His next words confirmed the Doctor's worst suspicions. 'We find that we are… superior.'

The Doctor's mind seethed with alarm. This small squad of Ice Warriors, with or without their space vehicle, could devastate and dominate Earth – continent by continent – if they chose to! And he had a definite feeling that this would have been part of that original Martian plan, conceived so many centuries ago, and halted only by a freak landing on that prehistoric glacier. Suppose there were other scout ships, buried in the ice? Varga mustn't be given the chance to put his secret orders into practice – which meant there was only one way out, dreadful but necessary. He began speaking with what seemed an unnecessary loudness – but not for Victoria's benefit. Clent had to be persuaded to act – and act now!

'You do realise,' stated the Doctor emphatically, 'that at a certain point – almost immediately, in fact – my Base will have to activate the Ioniser *regardless of the consequences*?'

Zondal didn't catch the urgent emphasis. He sneered in disbelief. 'And risk destroying you – and themselves? They are not fools!'

'Better that,' the Doctor started to say, 'than—'

In a flash, Varga's fist had grabbed his arm, exposed the tiny communicator and wrenched the device free, switching it off in the process. He examined it closely, then laughed.

'A communicator! How useful!'

The Doctor had always known the risk of discovery. Realising what he had been trying to do, Victoria gasped in fear of Varga's retaliation. Neither of them expected his response.

'When the time is right,' hissed the warlord arrogantly, 'we will use this device ourselves.' He stepped closer to the Doctor.

'You have been most helpful, Doctor. You will forgive my interruption of your warning to your friends. Shall I complete it for you?' He laughed cruelly. '*Better that than… be conquered by these Martians!* And you are right!' He gestured towards the engine complex, and his next words struck fear into both the Doctor and Victoria.

'There is one thing we need to complete our power,' hissed the Martian arrogantly. 'Then we shall be invincible – and this planet will be ours to conquer as we please!'

8

The Martian Ultimatum

Leader Clent stared at the blank video screen and said nothing for several seconds. It seemed that – with the Doctor's message ending so abruptly – their last chance had vanished.

'What can we do?' asked Jan. 'The Doctor! We've got to help him!'

Clent shook his head. 'You heard what he said. Regardless of the consequences, he wants us to take the risk and use the Ioniser.' He frowned. 'But he's not only offering himself as a sacrifice – it's us as well!'

'If only he could have said more... Perhaps he means the spaceship's reactor *isn't* dangerous?'

'But the aliens *are*...' replied the Leader grimly. 'It's no good guessing, Miss Garrett. We must have facts!'

She had to agree. 'Until we programme the computer with the correct information, it cannot instruct us how to act.'

Clent turned back to the Ioniser monitors. They were stable, but almost dormant at half power. 'If only the Ioniser would hold...'

'At present output, it's steadily losing ground to the glacier.' Inside her mind, a silent voice shouted Jan's real opinions. Forget the glacier! Do something to save the Doctor and the girl! We owe them that much! We cannot let them die! Aloud she said, 'We dare not increase power... not yet.'

Clent turned to her. She sensed the deep confusion in his mind. He was torn between duty, humanity and the need for action – knowing that whatever decision he took, the result could spell disaster... Suddenly, the computer hummed into life.

'*World Director, Ionisation Programme, to all sectors. The new control equation originating from Brittanicus Base will be adapted to conditions prevailing in each sector, and linked to World Central Control. On central command pulse, a concerted intercontinental attack on the glaciers will commence in six hours exactly. Report readiness in three hours. Leaders to confirm status report one hour to zero. Message ends.*'

Jan turned desperately to Clent. 'We can't do it!' she cried hopelessly.

Clent's face was stern; like a soldier taking orders in the face of imminent destruction, he knew instinctively that he must act without question. 'If we don't act, the world plan must fail! We have no choice, Miss Garrett!'

Jan was too well trained to defy her superior, but she clutched desperately at one last straw... 'The computer *must* be told,' she insisted firmly, 'as a matter of procedure.' As Clent started to protest, she added quickly, 'With the fresh directive from World Control, it may be able to resolve our local situation.' She was relying desperately on Clent's addiction to the rule-book and, to her relief, he nodded in reluctant agreement.

'Very well, Miss Garrett, feed the relevant data to ECCO, if you must.' But at the back of his mind he instinctively knew what the computer would say in answer to the grim dilemma. There was only one reply it could give – and that answer would save no one. Seconds later it gave its response.

'As instructed, set up all circuits to the new equation. No action to be taken until further data available regarding potential nuclear explosion. Prepare to notify World Control in event of unresolved emergency. Repeat, take no action!' The machine fell silent.

Clent looked across at Jan. 'It's what we both expected, isn't it,' he commented wearily. 'But the computer must be obeyed. We must wait.'

'In five hours from now, you have to report that we are in emergency status!' exclaimed Jan. 'At least we have that much time!'

Clent studied her tense face, and saw she didn't understand. 'Miss Garrett, you still don't realise the logic of the computer's decision not to act, do you?'

Puzzled, she shook her head. 'The computer can only ever be logical. It hasn't enough facts – it told us so a moment ago.'

Clent's reply carried an undertone of despair. 'We have just asked the computer if it is prepared to commit suicide. If we use the Ioniser and we explode the alien reactor, the Base – and the computer – will be destroyed. If we do *not* use the Ioniser, the glaciers will advance and destroy the Base. Either way, its survival is at risk – and one of its prime directives, programmed as a vital part of its basic circuitry, is to survive! Now do you see the dilemma?'

Jan was silent. It wasn't only the computer's dilemma, she realised; it was Clent's as well. Whatever he did, failure was staring him in the face.

'We can at least evacuate,' she said quietly, knowing what his reaction would be. 'There's still time...'

Clent was shocked, and angry. 'Retreat? Throw in the towel? Perhaps you would be happy to face world opinion afterwards, Miss Garrett. I would not!'

'Is that all that matters? It isn't only your reputation at stake. There are the lives of—'

Jan stopped in mid-sentence as the picture of Walters flashed on to the video screen. His brisk message startled both Jan and Clent into action.

'Security to Leader Clent. Two emergency arrivals, sir. I've had them both brought to the medicare centre for treatment. One of them's Scientist Penley!'

Zondal was supervising the removal of the sonic cannon from its usual mounting inside the spaceship to a traction unit in the cave outside. Varga turned to the Doctor.

'As you can see, Doctor, we have more than just personal destructors!' He pointed to the weapon on his arm, and Victoria shuddered, remembering vividly the horror of that deadly gun. 'This can destroy a man in an instant – but the sonic cannon is capable of wiping out whole cities!'

'What's it to be used for?' asked the Doctor.

'It is an ultimatum,' hissed Varga. He laughed brutally. 'An ultimatum that accepts only one kind of reply – agreement!'

'But why?' asked Victoria bravely. 'You've already got us as hostages!'

'Yes,' agreed the Doctor. 'What else do you want?'

'Information,' said Varga. 'You have asked enough questions. Now you will provide answers…'

'I've already told you all I know about the Ioniser,' replied the Doctor. 'You don't need to worry—'

'What is its power source then? Tell me that!'

Suddenly the Doctor saw the situation in all its clarity. While he had been desperate to know what sort of reactor the Martians had on their spacecraft, they had realised that the Base might be the source of vital fuel for their reactor! The truth was, they were as helpless as Clent and the scientists – the perfect stalemate. But a distant groaning from the glacier outside reminded him of that one random factor. The moving river of ice was dependent on no one; unless it was stopped soon, the Ioniser Base would be swept away like every other man-made object in the glacier's path.

'So that's what you need…' he said shrewdly, looking past Varga into the engine complex. 'Fuel – for your reactor. Without it, you'll never be able to break free!'

'Answer my question!' commanded the warlord, holding his sonic destructor close to Victoria's head, 'or the girl dies! Quickly!'

'And if I tell you?'

'We will take what we need, and use it to blast our way out of the glacier!' came the fierce reply. 'Speak!'

The Doctor looked suitably dejected. He turned from the engine complex to face Varga. 'Mercury isotopes – is that it?'

'You have them?' demanded the warlord eagerly.

Victoria's face filled with dismay at the Doctor's surrender to the Martian demands. 'Doctor, you shouldn't have told him!'

'You're more important, Victoria,' murmured the Doctor, then spoke to Varga defiantly. 'You won't find Leader Clent so easy to persuade! He's got a will as hard as granite!'

'The sonic cannon,' whispered Varga, 'can be programmed to disintegrate the hardest rock. This man will do as we ask – or we will smash his installation to pieces!' He pointed through the open doorway of the airlock.

There, at the entrance to the ice cave, pointing out over the hillside towards the Base, stood the sonic cannon. At Varga's gesture, Zondal stepped forward to the control panel inside the main complex of the spaceship. A video-radar screen, with a fire-path already plotted, was suspended over the gun controls.

'The weapon has only to be primed, and fired at my command,' hissed the warlord. 'Zondal is an expert bombardier. Let us hope he does not have to demonstrate his skills more than once!'

When Clent and Miss Garrett arrived in the medicare centre, Jamie was already encased in the computerised diagnostic chamber. Penley, who was overseeing its purring function, didn't seem to hear Clent enter. But when he did turn round to acknowledge the Leader's sour greeting, his expression was one of deep relief.

'So you've come back!' commented Clent.

'Of my own free will,' replied the renegade scientist. 'Largely because I was talked into it by that chap the

Doctor – and this young friend of his.'

'Is that all you expect?' jibed Clent. 'Free medical treatment? Don't think you'll be reinstated! You're an outsider – self-declared!'

Jan was examining Jamie. 'What's wrong with him?' she asked Penley anxiously. He smiled in reply, appreciating that she didn't share Clent's anger.

'He was shot by the warriors' guns,' Penley answered soberly, 'when they killed Arden. I was afraid there'd be some neural damage, but the diagnosis says it'll only be temporary – given the right treatment,' he added challengingly. 'Or will you try and put a stop to that, too?'

Walters, hovering in the background, looked uneasy. All the signs pointed to yet another row between the two scientists. Clent gestured Walters to remain.

'Stay here, Walters,' he ordered, 'you may be needed.'

'I'm not liable to be violent!' snapped Penley. 'I'm here to make sure that this lad gets the attention he needs – that's all. Besides which, there's this chap the Doctor—'

'Where is he?' asked Jan quickly. 'We lost contact with him over an hour ago. Have you seen him?'

Penley nodded, then threw an acid glance at Clent, who glowered back at him fiercely. 'He's up to something inside the alien spaceship. Trying to save your skin, I suppose!' Clent stiffened, but Penley continued. 'What are you going to do about him then?'

'There is nothing we can do,' announced Clent. 'The computer has given its instructions.'

Instantly, Penley flared into anger. 'You haven't changed have you? Can't you ever think for yourself? It won't fall apart because you tell it to mark time for a couple of hours!'

Clent's reply was cool and smug. 'We *are* marking time – at the request of the computer itself. For once,' smirked Clent, pleased to score over Penley's incessant jibing at the computer's authority, 'you and the computer are in agreement!'

'In that case, something's badly wrong. Has it got indigestion – or mumps even?' he asked hopefully.

Jan replied, trying desperately to keep the peace. If only these two would sink their petty differences and co-operate, she thought, their problems would be solved in no time!

'The spaceship may contain a reactor system that could explode under the effect of the full Ioniser impact,' she said simply. 'We daren't use it. But World Control have ordered us—'

'I know about the spaceship's reactor,' Penley replied. 'Didn't anybody have the sense to work out the time needed for isotope degeneration? For all we know, it may be perfectly harmless…' He turned to Clent, no longer joking. 'Now there's a sensible job for your computer, Clent.'

Clent almost snarled with rage. 'I have no intention of diverting the Base computer from its official programme!' he shouted. 'Least of all for something so trivial and irrelevant! The computer's judgement is quite clear—'

Penley started shouting back. 'Clent – you're a fool! Not even a man – just a slave to that stupid machine!'

'We all know your sort of freedom, Penley!' replied Clent savagely. 'Freedom to run away: from responsibility, from loyalty, from service to the community.'

'At least I have a mind of my own! I dare to act – but you dare *not*!' He grasped hold of Clent's arm. The gesture wasn't in any way violent, but Clent tore himself free and shouted at the security sergeant:

'Walters! Use your tranquilliser gun! Shoot!'

Instinctively and swiftly, Walters obeyed. The numbing drug took effect almost immediately. Penley slumped, unconscious, to the floor. As Walters holstered his gun and lifted the limp body on to a nearby bed-trolley, Clent caught Jan's look of disgust.

'I had no choice!' the Leader protested. 'You saw him grab me!' Jan said nothing. Everyone present knew the truth – including Clent. He turned to Walters, defensively. 'Strap him down,' he ordered. Clent ushered Jan towards the door. 'We have work to do...' he declared. But Jan stood fast, her face cold and determined. She pointed towards Jamie, still unconscious and cocooned inside the diagnostic unit.

'What about the boy?' she demanded, her tone daring Clent to ignore his condition. Clent glanced towards Jamie's helpless form; his face softened slightly. He stepped to the control panel of the machine, and pressed a brief sequence of coloured, illuminated tabs. The machine took on a new hum of increased activity, and a status panel now read TREATMENT IN PROGRESS.

'The machine will do the rest,' said Clent calmly. 'We must go back to the Ioniser Room and wait.' As she and the others left the laboratory, Jan threw one last glance back at Penley, drugged and pinioned. She couldn't help feeling that with he and the Doctor out of action, all hope had faded...

Varga's voice rasped harshly from the spaceship's loudspeaker system, bringing Zondal and his prisoners sharply to alert.

'I am at the perimeter of the Earthling Base! Prepare the sonic cannon for firing!'

Zondal's mighty fist touched the response switch. 'Pulse amplifier in operation now,' he replied to his unseen master.

Unseen by Zondal, the Doctor mimed a tearful face to Victoria. She responded by bursting into tears. As the Doctor drew the sobbing girl to his shoulder in gentle sympathy, Zondal turned briefly to them, and sneered.

'It's all right, Victoria,' murmured the Doctor comfortingly, 'you mustn't be afraid...'

'When Varga, our warlord, returns in victory,' declared the Ice Warrior proudly, 'then you will have cause for weeping!' He turned back to the complex process under his control, having no inkling of the furtive conversation which was being carried on behind his back. The Doctor handed a large handkerchief to Victoria. In its folds nestled one of the phials he had dialled from the Base dispenser. She looked surprised, but continued to sob aloud.

'Come along, my dear, have a good blow,' said the Doctor, then continued in a whisper, 'When I give the word, throw this stuff into Zondal's face!'

'What is it?' Victoria asked between sobs.

'Ammonium sulphide.'

Ammonium sulphide?' Victoria blinked. 'But that's what they use for making stink bombs, isn't it?'

'I can see you've had a sound English education,' the Doctor commented. 'You're quite right – in fact, it's a minor poisonous gas. Unpleasant, but harmless to humans.' He threw a quick glance at the hulking Martian. 'But to aliens – quite possibly deadly.'

The shrill whine of power had reached such a pitch that it was now virtually inaudible to human ears. Zondal activated his radio-link, and reported. 'Pulse amplified and held,' he hissed. 'Ready to fire.'

'Good, Zondal,' replied Varga. 'I will now contact the scientists. On my command, you will fire – once. Do you understand?'

'Understood, Commander.'

Suddenly, Victoria cried out in alarm.

'Doctor! Look! There's water coming into the spaceship!'

'Great heavens!' exclaimed the Doctor, beckoning the Ice Warrior across. 'Do you realise what this means, Zondal? The ship is breaking up under the ice!'

Caught between staying at his firing post, and investigating a possible disaster, Zondal hesitated – and was lost.

'What is it?' he asked suspiciously. 'Do not try to trick me!' Then, as he peered to see what the Doctor was indicating, Victoria threw the contents of the phial straight into his face. For a second, the liquid had no effect at all. Victoria glanced at the Doctor in horrified dismay. Then, just as Zondal seemed to be recovering from the puny attack, his sonic pistol poised for action, the toxic fumes began to grip the creature's throat. He lurched and fell, choking, to his knees. The Doctor poured the contents of his own phial on to Zondal's bowed and retching head, and then, like Victoria, skipped nimbly out of range. But even as they watched, the Martian's body convulsed into a helpless wreck. Varga's harsh voice rang out again.

'Zondal! Fire – now!'

The stern command had the momentary effect of pulling the desperately weakened warrior back from the edge of oblivion. Zondal lunged weakly towards the control panel, reaching for the firing button. The Doctor dashed forward – but he was too late. Zondal's fist struck home, and the cannon fired!

9

Counter-Attack

The blast struck the control room without warning. Clent and Miss Garrett were hurled to the floor. Clent's first thought was that there had been a localised earthquake – but a quick glance at the seismic chart gave no indication of a natural disaster. He and Jan had barely risen to their feet, half-stunned, when Walters burst into the control room, dusty and battered.

'Sir—' he gasped. He paused to steady himself.

'For heaven's sake, Walters,' demanded Clent, 'what's happening?'

'The documentation wing, sir' – explained the security sergeant breathlessly – 'it's gone – blown apart!'

They stared at him in disbelief. Then a glimmer of understanding crept into Clent's brain. 'We're under attack!' he whispered wildly. 'But who on earth…'

Suddenly, the videoscreen flicked into life. Partially distorted by interference, but hideously recognisable, was the grim face of the Ice Warrior.

'Leader Clent,' came the terrifying hiss, 'you are at my mercy. Obey me, or you will be destroyed!'

Clent snapped back, hysterically defiant. 'I refuse! You cannot destroy us!'

'You do not believe me? Must I fire again?'

Clent turned towards the others, but hardly seemed to see them. His eyes looked glazed; he rubbed his hands together in nervous desperation. Jan suddenly felt an enormous surge of pity – he was on the verge of losing his nerve completely.

'What can we do?' he croaked, looking about him aimlessly. Suddenly, his eyes brightened. 'We must play for time!' Walters was more realistic.

'The building won't take any more like that, sir! There's men killed already.'

'Then we'll talk to them,' snapped Clent, and, acting with a little of his old authority, he addressed the image on the videoscreen. 'Exactly who am I speaking to?' Jan moved forward and stood by his shoulder.

'My name is Varga, warlord of Mars. I order you to surrender – or you will die!'

'You will gain nothing by destroying us,' replied Clent. 'We both have urgent needs. But I will agree to talk – nothing more.' At first, the Martian didn't reply. The tension became almost unbearable.

'If I come in peace,' the voice replied at last, 'there must be trust between us. No treachery!'

'There will be no traps – or conditions,' declared Clent.

'See that you keep to that,' rasped Varga, and his image faded from the screen.

It took several minutes for the scientists to regain their normal composure.

'What does he want…' whispered Jan.

'My men don't stand a chance against weapons like that, sir,' insisted the security sergeant. 'It'd be murder!'

'That wasn't in my mind, Walters,' retorted Clent. 'You heard what he said – no treachery!'

'But can we trust him?' asked Jan.

'We have to, don't we?' replied Clent. 'He has… certain advantages – like the ability to blast us and this whole building apart!'

'We could try bluffing him,' suggested Jan seriously. 'He doesn't know about the computer's command to hold back. We could threaten to destroy the glacier and his ship with it!'

Before Clent could answer, Walters stepped forward, his face eager. 'Better than that, sir, why don't we do it anyway? It's our only chance of survival—'

Miss Garrett turned on the burly security commander. 'There are human lives at stake there, man: the girl's and the Doctor's! We *can* only bluff!'

'We will not use the Ioniser,' clipped the Leader firmly, 'unless the computer authorises it!'

'Don't tell me about that damned machine!' shouted Walters. 'What's your precious computer ever given us, Clent? Nothing! Nothing but trouble! And it's time somebody put an end to it!' He dragged his tranquilliser gun from its holster, and was about to use it to smash the sleek head of ECCO. Suddenly Clent cried out, and pointed towards the open doorway.

'Walters!'

The wild-eyed security commander spun to face the intruders, gun in hand. His eyes widened at the sight of

141

Varga and his three warriors. It was the last thing he ever saw. Almost instantaneously, Varga's men reacted to the sight of Walters' weapon with a concerted burst of sonic fire-power. The burly man fell, his face horribly contorted with pain.

As Jan stifled a scream of terror, Clent stared dully at the body.

'So much for trust…' hissed the warlord.

'That wasn't planned!' protested Clent. 'He wasn't going to harm you – it was the computer that he wanted to smash!'

'I do not need your explanations,' responded Varga. 'Our truce is at an end!' As the Martian strode into the control complex and began studying its equipment and layout, Jan had the distinct feeling that the truce was never intended to be kept. This alien was ruthless; unless they were careful, Walters would not be the last to die. She motioned to the few remaining technical operators to do nothing to antagonise the Martians. One glance showed her that they were not likely to make even a token resistance.

'What is it you want?' Jan boldly asked.

Varga looked at her arrogantly. 'I have one major need; mercury isotopes for my spaceship's reactor. You will give them to me.'

Clent frowned, and intervened cautiously. 'But… we don't use mercury isotopes.'

'The Doctor stated that you had what we need – here! Do not try to trick me!'

'He was wrong – we have none,' answered Clent simply. 'What good would lying do?'

The warlord glowered at Clent, then moved towards Jan. He spoke gently, but the menace in his voice was unmistakable.

'Tell me,' he whispered smoothly, 'what will happen if we shut off your reactor in order to extract the fuel elements that we need?'

'You can't do that!' Jan answered in alarm. 'It powers everything: heat, light—'

'And the Ioniser...' hissed the Martian. 'Without the reactor, you would be completely at the mercy of the glacier.'

'You don't realise the dangers!' Clent exclaimed, his face pale with stress. 'The power source is locked in directly with the Ioniser. If you cut out the energy pulse before it reduces to safety level, the feed-back effect will blast you and this building into a state of ion-flux!'

The warlord studied him briefly, then moved across to examine the Ioniser control panel. 'What is its temperature range?' he hissed, his great fists poised above the controls.

'Don't touch it!' cried Clent. 'It's fully primed!' Varga's hand fell back, but his arrogant head turned towards Clent, waiting for the answer. 'It can melt rock,' muttered Clent reluctantly.

'It can volatise rock!' the Martian was obviously impressed. 'What a weapon!'

'It isn't a weapon!' insisted Clent nervously. 'It's a scientific instrument!'

'But highly dangerous,' interjected Jan, 'unless it's handled correctly. You do so at your own risk,' she added.

'You are its operator?' hissed Varga, then taking her nod

of assent as answer, continued, 'You will take it down to safety level. Now!'

Jan looked towards Clent. His shoulders slumped; he nodded wearily in agreement. But Jan hadn't given in completely yet. 'It'll take some time,' she said.

'Do not attempt to trick me,' rasped the Martian. 'I know that you are afraid its heat will explode my ship. If you make one false move…' he placed his sonic destructor at Jan's head '… you will be the first to die!'

Clent stepped forward to defend Jan. Varga's gun swung in his direction. He strove to hide his fear. 'Miss Garrett is the only person who is qualified to disconnect the Ioniser safely! If you kill her—'

Varga moved closer to the Leader. 'And what exactly do you do here?' he asked softly. A little of Clent's old dignity returned. 'I am in charge of this establishment, with the official rank of Leader.'

The Martian coughed out his menacing laugh, and placed the sonic weapon at Clent's ear. 'Then you have less value to me than your colleague, who has more valuable skills.' The warlord looked at Jan; her eyes showed her fear. 'To kill this man, your Leader,' he hissed, 'would be no loss to me. Do you wish to see him die?'

'No!' cried Jan. 'Please!'

'Then do as I say! Close down the machine as quickly as is safely possible!' Varga brutally thrust the sonic weapon against Clent's cheek, making him howl with pain. 'Or your Leader will be destroyed!'

Zondal had been so affected by the toxic gas that he was

likely to remain in a deep coma for hours. Victoria kept glancing at the sprawled, massive body nervously – but the Doctor was wholly concentrating on adapting the intricate mechanism of the sonic cannon's control panel to a purpose all his own.

'But what is it you're trying to do?' asked Victoria.

'It's a bit difficult to explain, Victoria,' replied the Doctor, without pausing. 'You see, this weapon works on the basis that sound waves cause the objects in their path to reverberate.'

'The objects vibrate in sympathy,' nodded Victoria. 'I know. Father told me about it once.'

The Doctor frowned at a particularly involved piece of circuitry, then carried on. 'Well, if you can produce an unsympathetic vibration, severe damage results…'

'Damage?' asked Victoria, then added brightly, 'Like when a singer hits a note that breaks glass?'

'That's it – only the Ice Warriors make it happen to the neural and cell systems of the human body. My plan is to change the frequency of this gun's pulse rate so that it affects the Martians, and not us – to frequency seven, I think.'

'Frequency seven? What will that do?'

'Primarily, it affects liquids. And I've got a theory that the Martians' cells contain a much larger fluid content than ours.' He stood back, apparently satisfied, then rubbed his chin thoughtfully.

'But you're not sure.' Her eyes widened in alarm.

The Doctor nodded soberly. 'There are bound to be side-effects,' he agreed, 'but the warriors should get the worst of it. You see, their helmets will trap and intensify the sound waves – in fact I'm banking on that!'

'You mean it'll knock the Martians out,' asked Victoria tentatively, 'but just leave the scientists a bit dizzy?'

The Doctor carefully replaced the casing of the control panel. Victoria could tell from his face and the hesitation in his reply that he wasn't at all happy.

'Or can something go wrong?' she demanded.

He looked her straight in the eyes, and gave her an honest answer. 'Human brain cells also contain a high percentage of liquid. Unless I'm very careful, the effect on our friends could be fatal.'

Jan stepped back from the Ioniser controls, her face bitter with defeat. 'It's done – operating at minimal status.' She looked at Clent – but found no response there. It was as though he was in a world of his own. 'The ice is already advancing.' She pointed to the chart. Varga wasn't interested in the glacier.

'Disconnect the machine totally!' he barked.

With no alternative but to do as he commanded, Jan opened the power connector and the machine died. Its pitch sank to a feeble drone.

'Now the reactor!' ordered the warlord.

'Not until all residual power has drained off!' replied Jan sternly. 'You know the danger!'

'You will regret this, Varga,' Clent declared, strangely calm. 'You cannot fight the whole world!'

'Your world is nothing!' hissed Varga contemptuously. 'We will live to regret only that my superiors on Mars cannot congratulate us.' He gestured abruptly towards Jan. 'Hurry!'

All eyes, Martian and human, were on the dying machine. No one noticed the ragged form that had hidden so skilfully in the shadows outside the doorway to the control room, and who watched with dismay the fateful situation in which Clent and Jan were trapped. Penley had woken from the effects of the tranquilliser gun to find himself strapped down to the trolley in the medicare laboratory. It had been minutes before he realised that whoever had fastened the restrainers had left them cunningly half-caught. It had been an easy task to unloose them and set himself free. Jamie, cocooned within the healing confines of the diagnostic unit, was unconscious but seemed, Penley noted, to be improving rapidly.

But Clent was a different matter – somehow, he had to be made to see that what he was doing could only end in disaster. It wasn't until Penley reached the vestibule outside the control room and realised just how desperate the situation was, that he felt a genuine respect for Clent's courage. It would have broken a lesser man. Faced with not only death but the destruction of all he held to be of importance in his scientific career, the Leader remained quietly defiant… and utterly helpless.

But so am I, thought Penley to himself. These Martians seemed invincible! Silently, he drew back into the shadowed corner to think – and in doing so, jarred his shoulder against a control box. Irritated, he glared at the unit – then looked again, wild thoughts racing through his mind. It was an air-conditioning stabiliser. At present set on automatic, with pre-set limits, it could also be converted to manual. His mouth dry, Penley's fingers fumbled rapidly to open up the casing; his mind swiftly assessed what he knew about the Martians. It was the boldly labelled status gauges that had triggered his thoughts: temperature, oxygen ratio, and humidity. These aliens were entirely at home in such Ice Age conditions as might exist on certain parts of their home planet, Mars. Well, thought Penley, we'll soon put an end to that! Switching the controls to manual, he increased all three elements to maximum – and prayed.

The effect was almost instantaneous. Rintan, the warrior standing closest to an air-conditioning grille in the control room, started to reel. The floor was rising and falling beneath him like a sinking ship! His great fists clawed at his throat, and his usually softly wheezing breath changed to a series of great tearing sobs. Within seconds, the humans, too, felt the increased surge of toxic heat – but still threatened by the warriors' weapons, they looked on helplessly as each of the Martians struggled to remain conscious. Only Varga kept any degree of keen awareness. He whirled to confront Clent furiously.

'What have you done to us!' he snarled. 'You have tricked us! For that you will die!'

But even as he raised his gun, a new terror struck. An immense, pulsing throb of sound filled the room – and its effect on the Martians was even more astounding than that of the heat. The humans slumped lifeless to the floor, like stones. The effect on the Martians was more terrifying. The sound flooded over them, through them – but, worst of all, it seemed to penetrate their great helmets. Crying out

148

hoarsely, lurching in agony, there was no escape from the relentless sound that threatened to crush their very brains... Then, just as suddenly, the sonic terror ended.

But the combined effect of the sound and the atmospheric assault – which still hadn't stopped – had left the warriors, Varga included, in a state of confusion and shock. Then, even as they still recovered, the voice of the Doctor came through on Varga's personal communicator.

'Varga! This is the Doctor. Will you retreat – or shall I use frequency seven again?'

Nearly out of his mind with pain and anger, Varga still registered that deadly number: Frequency Seven. Used in the prisons of his home planet as a form of aversion punishment, continuous doses of it could destroy the brain, leaving the body a living vegetable. How did the Doctor know this?

'Varga!' came that relentless voice once more. 'Answer – or I fire again!'

There was no other choice but to obey. With a furious, sweeping gesture, the warlord ordered his warriors from the building. Furious, Varga shouted aloud the message to the Doctor: 'You will suffer for this!' Then, lurching past the crumpled body of the human in the vestibule outside, the Ice Warriors streamed out into the freedom of the snowy wastes – and the protection of their spaceship.

But when they reached the ice cavern, they discovered the sonic cannon fused and destroyed, Zondal unconscious, and both their prisoners gone...

10

On the Brink of Destruction!

Jamie, who had just recovered consciousness, was helped out of the snug confines of the diagnostic unit by an almost hysterically relieved Victoria. The Doctor had gone on ahead to the control room without explanations. He had told the two youngsters to follow as soon as possible.

'What's been happening?' asked Jamie, stretching his cramped limbs. Then, as memories crowded back, he looked at Victoria more thoughtfully. 'Arden – is he—?'

She nodded quickly. Then, as they walked through the empty corridors to the control room, she filled in what had happened during Jamie's healing sleep, and what they might expect to find. On arrival, the Doctor quickly made it clear that there was no time for questions or answers. As he helped Penley to his feet, he indicated the reviving bodies of the scientists and technicians who were littered all over the control room floor.

'We've no time to waste. Help some of the others, will you?'

'That was rather a neat trick,' commented Penley. 'How did you do it?'

The Doctor smiled, mildly apologetic. 'Made a mess of the Ice Warriors' weapon system, I'm afraid. I'll tell you about it another time.'

Jan, quickly recovering, turned to the Doctor in dismay.

'The Ioniser – they made me disconnect it!'

'Then link it up again – fast as you can!'

Jan looked to Clent for confirmation. 'That'll be perfectly in line with the computer's directive, Miss Garrett. You may proceed.' Jan hurried to put his order into action. Clent turned to the Doctor, his tired face filled with relief. 'Thank you, Doctor,' he said, and then, seeing Penley standing at the Doctor's shoulder, frowned. 'You played your part as well, I gather,' he conceded. But his eyes still looked unfriendly.

'Clent' – the Doctor interjected urgently – 'the spaceship's reactor is ion-powered. Mercury isotopes—'

The Leader's face fell. One of the main reasons why the Base reactor didn't use mercury isotopes was that their critical fusion level had proved uncontrollable on a large scale. 'Then we dare not use the Ioniser at full force,' he said dejectedly. 'It's our last chance gone…'

'You still haven't taken the degeneration factor into account!' exclaimed Penley.

'But there could still be enough residual particles to form a prolonged chain reaction!' barked Clent. 'Don't you understand the risk? We could all be wiped out in an instant!'

'It's a risk you have to take,' insisted the Doctor. 'If you don't, the Base will go down under the glaciers anyway.'

'Not forgetting the aliens,' Penley reminded them. There was a moment's pause as this threat sank in. Jan had brought the Ioniser into operation once more, and it hummed quietly in the background as she came to report.

'It's on minimal power, Leader Clent,' she said. 'We can use it at any time you want.'

Clent turned away, not wanting the others to see his fear. He knew the next step that must be taken – but he could only draw back.

'The computer said wait!' he stated vehemently.

Jan looked at him in surprise. 'It said wait until we had more information. We've got it now!'

'Can't you see it won't make any difference? It dare not act – *we* dare not act!'

'And why's that?' asked Jamie, who had overheard Clent's last outburst.

'Because, Jamie, the computer is faced with an insoluble problem,' explained the Doctor. 'Either way, the computer risks destroying itself – and that it cannot do. It can only play safe.'

'But if it does nothing…' faltered Jamie, '… that's just as bad!'

'Exactly,' came Penley's quiet voice. 'Which leaves us only one course of action.'

'If you think I'm going to evacuate—' Clent started to shout.

'My dear chap, you haven't got time for that,' replied Penley. 'It isn't a question of logic any more. It's a question of world survival. You must over-ride the computer.'

Clent looked at his former colleague, and shook his head. 'You're mad! You want to kill us all. There has to be another way!'

'I want to survive,' rapped Penley. 'And I'm willing to take the risk that your pet machine daren't! That's what men are for, Clent! That's what Leaders like you are for!' He tried to appeal to the man who had once been his friend. 'Be brave, Clent. Be yourself!'

'But what about the World plan? If we act too soon, it'll be as bad as being too late! We must act at the appointed hour, and not before!'

'It's *our* problem – not World Control's!' insisted Penley. 'It's us that's out of step, not them – and they haven't got aliens on their doorstep as well as the glacier! Unless we deal with them now, world civilisation is going to find itself involved in interplanetary war!'

'Someone must decide – and quickly,' agreed the Doctor. He looked into Clent's face. The Leader seemed almost incapable of words – let alone action.

'Such a decision…' muttered the Leader, then bent his head, unable to look the others in the face. 'I can't,' he said.

The Doctor glanced at Miss Garrett. She shook her head and nodded towards Penley – as the Doctor hoped she would.

'It's up to you, Penley,' declared the Doctor, seriously.

The transference of authority stung Clent into one last typical act.

'I demand the right to consult the computer!' he cried, moving towards ECCO; without waiting for agreement or argument, he formally addressed the sleek head. 'Problem – in addition to previous data, include the factor that the alien spaceship is powered by an ion reactor. Dare we use the Ioniser? What are the alternatives? Answer!'

The reply shocked everyone – but Clent most of all. Instead of its usual swift, objective appraisal and cold-blooded judgement, the tortured machine spluttered forth a stream of gibberish, half electronic, half verbal – and all totally incoherent. As its smooth head jerked from side to side in spasmodic twitches, a pungent whiff of overloaded circuits drifted from its control panel, and Clent, realising the impossible dilemma facing the machine, switched it off.

'It's gone out of its mind!' exclaimed Jamie. 'It can't cope!'

As Clent slumped listlessly into a nearby chair, Penley took command, firmly but quietly. 'Miss Garrett, inform World Control. We're using the Ioniser now – and tell them precisely why. Full report to follow – we hope.'

Victoria suddenly remembered what the Martian warlord had said to the Doctor. A look of alarm crossed her face. 'The Martian spaceship!' she exclaimed. 'If you free it from the ice!'

The possibility of the Martians freely roaming the sky gripped them all with a sense of doom. What other terrifying weapons did that vehicle possess? How could they combat such a threat? It was Clent's tired voice that supplied the answer.

'I told Varga that the Ioniser was a scientific instrument capable of melting rock,' he said calmly. 'But he saw it as a weapon.' He paused, and studied Penley intently. 'I suggest... that it should be used as such.'

For a moment, all eyes were on the two top scientists. Each weighed the bitter consequences of his calling, and pondered upon the grim decision that he must take. Then Penley nodded, and spoke with an air of quiet purpose.

'It has to be done,' he said and, moving to the Ioniser controls, began to raise its operating pitch to maximum power...

Zondal had expected the harshest of punishments for his dismal failure. With the sonic cannon wrecked and useless, and his prisoners escaped, he had knelt before Varga, only taking consolation from the fact that the finality of his punishment would at least remove the disgrace.

But defeat at the hands of the Earthlings had thrust all thoughts of a court martial out of the warlord's mind. The most urgent need was to be ready to break free when the ice started to melt – for he was certain now that the Earthlings would use the Ioniser, whatever the risk. So Zondal had been spared, but for one purpose only.

'We have to escape before the floods overcome us, Zondal!' hissed the Martian leader. 'It is your task to make our engines function – quickly!'

'But the fuel cells are almost useless!' replied his reprieved lieutenant. Then, aware that if he succeeded in raising the power they needed, his earlier mistake would be cancelled out, he declared vehemently, 'But I will try everything possible!'

He had tried every technical trick he knew, and other desperate experiments as well. But the most he had managed was to raise the power gauges trembling barely above the zero mark. In the cave outside, the ice groaned and shuddered in constant movements.

Isbur returned from a final reconnaissance outside, and closing the airlock for the last time, reported briefly. 'The ice is breaking up, Commander. The water is rising!'

Varga ordered his warriors to action stations, then moved to where Zondal was working frantically. 'Do you hear, Zondal?' he demanded harshly. 'But what use is freedom if we are helpless! Is there *no* life in the fuel elements?'

'I have not given up yet!' replied the engineer, then turned, as did Varga, in response to Isbur's sharp cry from the control room.

'Commander! Power!'

The warlord moved quickly to the control panel, followed closely by Zondal. It was true! The flickering needles were slowly rising, building towards operational level! Zondal stepped forward and grasped the controls. 'The ice is our friend.' He spoke in excitement. 'We still have power – and it is increasing!'

'Careful, Zondal,' hissed his commander. 'We must time the take-off boost perfectly. There will not be a second chance!'

And as the soft hum of power began to throb through the spaceship, Varga let his mind go forward to that moment when they would be free, in flight, and able to take a terrible revenge...

In the Ioniser control room, all eyes bar Penley's were glued to the electronic chart showing the glacier's advance. His glance never left the monitor screens and power dials of the machine which his hands were controlling. Jan Garrett was feeding him the relevant information about the state of the ice.

'Glacial front reduced by seven metres – par level of ten days ago now achieved!'

'We're winning!' exclaimed Victoria, almost hopping with excitement. But the Doctor's face was still grim.

'Not yet, Victoria,' he murmured. 'Not by a long chalk, I'm afraid. It isn't just the ice we've got to beat, remember.'

'Instrument readings on the ice face show a continuous rise in temperature. Still short of maximum,' continued Jan.

'How will we know?' asked Jamie. 'Those figures can't tell us what the Ice Warriors are up to, can they?'

Clent, standing in the background, answered Jamie's query patiently. 'The instruments on the ice face have the highest heat and shock resistance known to man,' he said. 'When they cease to function, everything about them will be destroyed – including the alien spacecraft.'

'And its reactor too?' Victoria asked the Doctor. He nodded. He didn't trouble to remind her that their own fate was also in the balance. There'd be little enough time to worry about that if disaster did strike!

Penley, his hand poised on the power lever, took a deep breath. 'Here we go,' he muttered tensely. 'All the way – now!' He rammed the throttle to full.

In the midst of chaos, Varga stood, majestic and alone. All about him, his warriors slid weakly to the floor, almost physically crushed by the combination of heat and humidity. Only Zondal remained conscious – close to collapse, he worked desperately at the smouldering controls. His choking voice barely reached Varga through the thick yellow fumes that were filling the ship. 'Must... achieve... lift-off!' were the Martian lieutenant's final gasping words. His commander looked down at his dying comrade and spoke words that Zondal never heard.

'It was not power in our engines, Zondal,' he rasped. 'It was the heat! Our greatest enemy: heat – from the Earthling's Ioniser!' Coughing from the fumes, he continued, 'A magnificent weapon!' Then, still standing, he saluted his dead comrades in the Martian style. 'No... surrender!' he cried as he, his ship and warriors, were blasted into infinity...

As Clent had predicted, all the seismic probe readings were dead – but the long-range seismograph print-out gave the minor blast recording that meant survival!

'Only a sub-tremor reading!' cried Jan, elated. 'We're safe! We've done it!'

'Miss Garrett—' responded Penley with a calm smile, 'perhaps you'd better set all circuits to automatic and tie in with World Control?'

Jan suddenly realised that several of the technicians were observing her happy outburst with amusement. With an embarrassed, apologetic smile, she moved to the Ioniser controls and made the correct connections. Penley approached Clent, who was sitting at the back of the room, his head in his hands.

'Clent, perhaps you'd care to check over the report we'll need to make?'

Clent looked up, surprised. He had expected only

scorn and humiliation from his colleagues. And now, of all people, it was Penley suggesting that they had a job to do – together! For a moment, Clent's face was blank and disbelieving. Then he smiled tiredly.

'Penley – you are the most insufferably irritating and infuriating person I have ever—' he stopped in mid-sentence, and then grinned broadly – 'been privileged to work with!'

Penley simply thrust out his hand to meet Clent's, and they held the grasp for a brief moment, 'Thanks, Clent...'

'Never could write a report, though, could you?' jibed the Leader gently, hiding his brief display of emotion. 'Don't worry, it's something I've been trained to do.'

'Without the computer?' twinkled Penley cheerfully.

'I think I can manage quite well, thank you...' declared Clent, then added – 'anyway, I can always get the Doctor to help out.' He turned to smile at the Doctor and his young friends – only to find they weren't anywhere to be seen. He turned back to Penley and Miss Garrett, his face puzzled. 'That's funny,' he said. 'Where on earth have they got to?'

Outside the great dome that protected Brittanicus Base, the snow had almost melted. Green shoots of long-covered grass were just beginning to show through on a mossy bank that had once been a snowdrift, and which still bore the imprint of a certain heavy, blue, twentieth-century police box.

But the box itself had long since gone...

About the Author

Brian Hayles

Born in England in 1930, Brian Hayles spent time in Canada as a sculptor and an art teacher before returning to Britain. He continued his career as a teacher for a while, writing in his spare time until he gave up the teaching to write full-time.

He wrote for radio, including many episodes of *The Archers*, as well as for television and film. As well as writing for various series such as *United!* and *Z Cars*, Hayles's work on *Doctor Who* included adventures for the first three Doctors. His first story was the well-remembered *The Celestial Toymaker*, though Hayles's scripts were extensively rewritten several times. After his historical adventure *The Smugglers*, Hayles wrote *The Ice Warriors* – introducing the creatures for which he is best remembered. He wrote three further Ice Warriors stories, the last two featuring the Third Doctor and set on the feudal planet Peladon.

Hayles's last work for television was the acclaimed children's serial *The Moon Stallion* – which starred Sarah Sutton, who later played *Doctor Who* companion Nyssa.

Brian Hayles died in 1978. His novel *Goldhawk* was published posthumously in 1979.

Doctor Who and the Ice Warriors
Between the Lines

Doctor Who and the Ice Warriors was originally published on 18 March 1976, almost a fortnight after 'The Seeds of Doom' had concluded *Doctor Who*'s thirteenth season of television adventures. It was the twenty-first of Target Books' novelisations, and the second by Brian Hayles, following the previous year's *Doctor Who and the Curse of Peladon*, also featuring the Ice Warriors.

The cover was by Chris Achilleos (Target had by this point dropped the internal illustrations from its *Doctor Who* range). This new edition re-presents the original 1976 publication. A few minor errors or inconsistencies have been corrected, but no attempt has been made to update or modernise the text – this is *Doctor Who and the Ice Warriors* as originally written and published.

This means that the novel retains certain stylistic and editorial practices that were current in 1975 (when the book was written and prepared for publication) but which have since adapted or changed.

Most obviously, measurements are mostly given in the then-standard imperial system of weights and measures: a yard is equivalent to 0.9144 metres; three feet make a yard, and a foot is 30 centimetres; twelve inches make a foot, and an inch is 25.4 millimetres. There's just one metric measurement, given by Miss Garrett as the Ioniser comes back under control; oddly, there was just the one metric measurement in the TV version, too, but a different one.

Doctor Who and the Ice Warriors sticks very closely to the scripts of Brian Hayles's televised episodes. The most noticeable change in the novelisation is that Hayles shifts several of the cliffhangers – Jamie's apparent death at the end of Chapter 5, for example, came several minutes before the end of Episode Three of the TV story. That episode instead ends with Victoria warning the Doctor and Clent about the Ice Warriors while Zondal prepares to fire on Brittanicus Base, events seen midway through Chapter 6 of this novelisation.

Brian Hayles had by this time written two television stories for the Third Doctor ('The Curse of Peladon' and 'The Monster of Peladon'). While his descriptions and characterisation of the Second Doctor are unmistakably Patrick Troughton, there are a few dialogue flourishes that are more suggestive of Jon Pertwee's incarnation. The Doctor can frequently be found addressing Clent as 'old chap' or 'my dear chap' and, on occasion, calling Jamie 'lad', neither of which is especially redolent of Troughton's Doctor (although Clent does get a single 'old chap' from him on screen in 'The Ice Warriors').

Clent (minus the walking stick used by actor Peter Barkworth) and the personnel of Brittanicus Base all closely resemble their television originals, although Jane Garrett is renamed Jan Garrett. Hayles also invents a new designation for the Base computer's communications unit – ECCO – that was never heard on screen.

In his television scripts, Hayles's description of the Ice Warriors makes no suggestion of any reptilian or lizard-like traits:

Inside the ice, distorted but recognisable, is what appears to be a helmeted warrior. The helmet is hood-like and ominous, in the style of that used under the opening titles of 'Hereward the Wake'. This is Varga.

Costume designer Martin Baugh, reasoning that an 'ice warrior' would be hard, cold and armoured, took upright crocodiles as the starting point for his design. The novelisation follows Baugh's design, with Hayles suggesting that each warrior's armour and weaponry is somehow 'part of the creature's physical anatomy'. He also makes full use of the Martians' breathless, hissing vocal delivery, something devised in rehearsals by actor Bernard Bresslaw, who had played Varga.

The transmission of 'The Ice Warriors' in 1967 followed on directly from 'The Abominable Snowmen'. When the TARDIS first arrives outside Brittanicus Base, Victoria notices the snow and Jamie wonders if they've landed on the same mountainside. This back reference to the previous story works considerably better in print, since 'The Abominable Snowmen' was set among the Tibetan mountains but filmed on the distinctly snow-free hillsides of North Wales. The Doctor also mentions Tibet, telling Clent that he and his companions have been on retreat there, though his further claim that they are 'sanctifiers' is dropped. (Terrance Dicks's novelisation, *Doctor Who and the Abominable Snowmen*, was published 16 months earlier, so there was continuity within the book range, too.)

One last – and minor – difference between broadcast story and print adventure comes when the Doctor is preparing to use his ammonium sulphide solution towards the end of Chapter 8. When Victoria identifies it as 'what they use for making stink bombs', the Doctor commends her 'sound English education'. On screen, this is 'a classical education', which is ironic – a sound English education in the Classics would not have left Victoria with the impression that Mars was the *Greek* god of war, as she seems to think in Chapter 3...

Here are details of other exciting Doctor Who *titles from BBC Books:*

DOCTOR WHO AND THE DALEKS
David Whitaker £4.99
ISBN 978 1 849 90195 6 **A First Doctor adventure**

With a new introduction by **NEIL GAIMAN**

'The voice was all on one level, without any expression at all, a dull monotone that still managed to convey a terrible sense of evil...'

The mysterious Doctor and his granddaughter Susan are joined by unwilling adventurers Ian Chesterton and Barbara Wright in an epic struggle for survival on an alien planet.

In a vast metal city they discover the survivors of a terrible nuclear war – the Daleks. Held captive in the deepest levels of the city, can the Doctor and his new companions stop the Daleks' plan to totally exterminate their mortal enemies, the peace-loving Thals? More importantly, even if they can escape from the Daleks, will Ian and Barbara ever see their home planet Earth again?

This novel is based on the second Doctor Who *story, which was originally broadcast from 21 December 1963 to 1 February 1964. This was the first ever* Doctor Who *novel, first published in 1964.*

DOCTOR WHO AND THE CRUSADERS

David Whitaker   £4.99

ISBN 978 1 849 90190 1   **A First Doctor adventure**

With a new introduction by **CHARLIE HIGSON**

*'I admire bravery, sir. And bravery and courage are clearly in
you in full measure. Unfortunately, you have no brains at all. I
despise fools.'*

Arriving in the Holy Land in the middle of the Third
Crusade, the Doctor and his companions run straight
into trouble. The Doctor and Vicki befriend Richard the
Lionheart, but must survive the cut-throat politics of the
English court. Even with the king on their side, they find
they have made powerful enemies.

Looking for Barbara, Ian is ambushed – staked out in the
sand and daubed with honey so that the ants will eat him.
With Ian unable to help, Barbara is captured by the cruel
warlord El Akir. Even if Ian escapes and rescues her, will
they ever see the Doctor, Vicki and the TARDIS again?

This novel is based on a Doctor Who *story which was originally
broadcast from 27 March to 17 April 1965, featuring the First
Doctor as played by William Hartnell, and his companions Ian,
Barbara and Vicki.*

DOCTOR WHO AND THE TENTH PLANET
Gerry Davis £4.99
ISBN 978 1 849 90474 2 **A First Doctor adventure**

With a new introduction by **TOM MacRAE**

'We were exactly like you once. Then our cybernetic scientists realised that our race was weakening. Our scientists and doctors invented spare parts for our bodies until we could be almost completely replaced.'

The TARDIS brings the Doctor and his friends to a space tracking base in the Antarctic – and straight into trouble. A space mission is going badly wrong, and a new planet has appeared in the sky.

Mondas, ancient fabled twin planet of Earth, has returned. Soon its inhabitants arrive. But while they used to be just like the humans of Earth, now they are very different. Devoid of emotions, their bodies replaced with plastic and steel, the Cybermen are here.

Humanity needs all the help it can get, but the one man who seems to know what's going on is terminally ill. As the Cybermen take over, the Doctor is dying…

This novel is based on the final story to feature the First Doctor, which was originally broadcast from 8 to 29 October 1966, featuring the First Doctor as played by William Hartnell in his very last adventure, and his companions Ben and Polly. This was the first Doctor Who *story to feature the Cybermen.*

DOCTOR WHO AND THE CYBERMEN
Gerry Davis   £4.99
ISBN 978 1 849 90191 8   **A Second Doctor adventure**

With a new introduction by **GARETH ROBERTS**

*'There are some corners of the universe which have bred the most
terrible things. Things which are against everything we have
ever believed in. They must be fought. To the death.'*

In 2070, the Earth's weather is controlled from a base on the
moon. But when the Doctor and his friends arrive, all is not
well. They discover unexplained drops of air pressure, minor
problems with the weather control systems, and an outbreak
of a mysterious plague.

   With Jamie injured, and members of the crew going
missing, the Doctor realises that the moonbase is under
attack. Some malevolent force is infecting the crew and
sabotaging the systems as a prelude to an invasion of Earth.
And the Doctor thinks he knows who is behind it: the
Cybermen.

This novel is based on 'The Moonbase', a Doctor Who *story which
was originally broadcast from 11 February to 4 March 1967,
featuring the Second Doctor as played by Patrick Troughton, and
his companions Polly, Ben and Jamie.*

DOCTOR WHO AND THE ABOMINABLE SNOWMEN
Terrance Dicks   £4.99
ISBN 978 1 849 90192 5   **A Second Doctor adventure**

With a new introduction by **STEPHEN BAXTER**

*'Light flooded into the tunnel, silhouetting the enormous shaggy
figure in the cave mouth. With a blood-curdling roar, claws
outstretched, it bore down on Jamie.'*

The Doctor has been to Det-Sen Monastery before, and
expects the welcome of a lifetime. But the monastery is a
very different place from when the Doctor last came. Fearing
an attack at any moment by the legendary Yeti, the monks
are prepared to defend themselves, and see the Doctor as a
threat.

   The Doctor and his friends join forces with Travers, an
English explorer out to prove the existence of the elusive
abominable snowmen. But they soon discover that these
Yeti are not the timid animals that Travers seeks. They are
the unstoppable servants of an alien Intelligence.

This novel is based on a Doctor Who *story which was originally
broadcast from 30 September to 4 November 1967, featuring
the Second Doctor as played by Patrick Troughton, and his
companions Jamie and Victoria.*

DOCTOR WHO AND THE AUTON INVASION
Terrance Dicks   £4.99
ISBN 978 1 849 90193 2   A Third Doctor adventure

With a new introduction by RUSSELL T DAVIES

'Here at UNIT we deal with the odd – the unexplained. We're prepared to tackle anything on Earth. Or even from beyond the Earth, if necessary.'

Put on trial by the Time Lords, and found guilty of interfering in the affairs of other worlds, the Doctor is exiled to Earth in the 20th century, his appearance once again changed. His arrival coincides with a meteorite shower. But these are no ordinary meteorites.

The Nestene Consciousness has begun its first attempt to invade Earth using killer Autons and deadly shop window dummies. Only the Doctor and UNIT can stop the attack. But the Doctor is recovering in hospital, and his old friend the Brigadier doesn't even recognise him. Can the Doctor recover and win UNIT's trust before the invasion begins?

This novel is based on 'Spearhead from Space', a Doctor Who story which was originally broadcast from 3 to 24 January 1970, featuring the Third Doctor as played by Jon Pertwee, with his companion Liz Shaw and the UNIT organisation commanded by Brigadier Lethbridge-Stewart.

DOCTOR WHO AND THE CAVE MONSTERS
Malcolm Hulke   £4.99
ISBN 978 1 849 90194 9   **A Third Doctor adventure**

With a new introduction by **TERRANCE DICKS**

'Okdel looked across the valley to see the tip of the sun as it sank below the horizon. It was the last time he was to see the sun for a hundred million years.'

UNIT are called in to investigate security at a secret research centre buried under Wenley Moor. Unknown to the Doctor and his colleagues, the work at the centre has woken a group of Silurians – intelligent reptiles that used to be the dominant life form on Earth in prehistoric times.

Now they have woken, the Silurians are appalled to find 'their' planet populated by upstart apes. The Doctor hopes to negotiate a peace deal, but there are those on both sides who cannot bear the thought of humans and Silurians living together. As UNIT soldiers enter the cave systems, and the Silurians unleash a deadly plague that could wipe out the human race, the battle for planet Earth begins.

This novel is based on 'The Silurians', a Doctor Who *story which was originally broadcast from 31 January to 14 March 1970, featuring the Third Doctor as played by Jon Pertwee, with his companion Liz Shaw and the UNIT organisation commanded by Brigadier Lethbridge-Stewart.*

DOCTOR WHO AND THE DAY OF THE DALEKS
Terrance Dicks £4.99
ISBN 978 1 849 90473 5   **A Third Doctor adventure**

With a new introduction by **GARY RUSSELL**

'You are the Doctor. You are an enemy of the Daleks! Now you are in our power! You will be exterminated! YOU WILL BE EXTERMINATED!'

UNIT is called in when an important diplomat is attacked in his own home – by a man who then vanishes into thin air. The Doctor and Jo spend a night in the 'haunted' house and meet the attackers – who have time-jumped back from the 22nd century in the hope of changing history.

Travelling forward in time, the Doctor and Jo find themselves trapped in a future world where humans are slaves and the Daleks have already invaded. Using their ape-like servants the Ogrons to maintain order, the Daleks are now the masters of Earth.

As the Doctor desperately works to discover what has happened to put history off-track, the Daleks plan a time-jump attack on the 20th century.

This novel is based on a Doctor Who *story which was originally broadcast from 1 to 22 January 1972, featuring the Third Doctor as played by Jon Pertwee, with his companion Jo Grant and the UNIT organisation commanded by Brigadier Lethbridge-Stewart.*

DOCTOR WHO – THE THREE DOCTORS
Terrance Dicks   £4.99
ISBN 978 1 849 90478 0   **A Third Doctor adventure**

With a new introduction by **ALASTAIR REYNOLDS**

The President of the Time Lords turned triumphantly to the Chancellor. 'You see, my Lord? We cannot help the Doctor, but perhaps he can help himself!'

A mysterious black hole is draining away power from the Universe. Even the Time Lords are threatened. The Doctor is also in trouble. Creatures from the black hole besiege UNIT Headquarters. The only person who can help the Doctor is… himself.

The Time Lords bring together the first three incarnations of the Doctor to discover the truth about the black hole and stop the energy drain.

The Doctors and their companions travel through the black hole itself, into a universe of anti-matter. Here they meet one of the very first Time Lords – Omega, who gave his race the power to travel through time.

Trapped for aeons in the black hole, he now plans to escape – whatever the cost.

This novel is based on a Doctor Who *story which was originally broadcast from 30 December 1972 to 20 January 1973, featuring the first three Doctors as played by William Hartnell, Patrick Troughton, and Jon Pertwee, together with Jo Grant and the UNIT organisation commanded by Brigadier Lethbridge-Stewart.*

DOCTOR WHO AND THE ARK IN SPACE
Ian Marter £4.99
ISBN 978 1 849 90476 6 **A Fourth Doctor adventure**

With a new introduction by **STEVEN MOFFAT**

'Homo Sapiens... what an indomitable species... it is only a few million years since it crawled up out of the sea and learned to walk... a puny defenceless biped... it has survived flood, plague, famine, war... and now here it is out among the stars... awaiting a new life.'

The survivors of a devastated future Earth lie in suspended animation on a great satellite. When Earth is safe again, they will awaken. But when the Doctor, Sarah and Harry arrive on the Terra Nova, they find the systems have failed and the humans never woke.

The Wirrrn Queen has infiltrated the satellite, and laid her eggs inside one of the sleepers. As the first of the humans wake, they face an attack by the emerging Wirrrn.

But not everyone is what they seem, and the only way the Doctor can discover the truth is by joining with the dead mind of the Wirrrn Queen. The price of failure is the Doctor's death, and the end of humanity.

This novel is based on a Doctor Who *story which was originally broadcast from 25 January to 15 February 1975, featuring the Fourth Doctor as played by Tom Baker, and his companions Sarah Jane Smith and Harry Sullivan.*

DOCTOR WHO AND THE LOCH NESS MONSTER
Terrance Dicks   £4.99
ISBN 978 1 849 90475 9   **A Fourth Doctor adventure**

With a new introduction by **MICHAEL MOORCOCK**

*Harry stared in amazement at the fierce head on the immensely
long neck, the huge body with its two low humps, and the flat,
powerful tail. 'We must be under Loch Ness,' he gasped. 'And that
thing – that's the monster!'*

Centuries ago, a Zygon spaceship crash landed in Loch Ness.
Now, with their home planet destroyed, the alien creatures
plan to take over Earth. Their most powerful weapon is a
huge armoured dinosaur-like creature of terrifying power
that they brought to Earth as an embryo – the Loch Ness
Monster.

The Doctor, Sarah and Harry soon discover that the
Zygons have another weapon. They can assume the identity
of any human they capture. Who knows which of their
friends might really be a Zygon?

UNIT faces one of its toughest battles as Broton, Warlord
of the Zygons, puts his plan into action and the Loch Ness
Monster attacks.

This novel is based on a Doctor Who *story which was originally
broadcast from 30 August to 20 September 1975, featuring the
Fourth Doctor as played by Tom Baker, with his companions Sarah
Jane Smith and Harry Sullivan and the UNIT organisation
commanded by Brigadier Lethbridge-Stewart.*